She closed her eyes, ⬛ exquisite millisecond⬛ brush of his lips over hers.

But she told herself she'd only imagined it.

The crowd had dispersed, caught up in another song, another dance, another moment. But Gracie couldn't quite let this moment go. And neither, it seemed, could he. When he began to lower his head toward hers—there was no mistaking his intention this time—she didn't know how to react. Not until his mouth covered hers completely. After that, she knew exactly what to do.

She kissed him back.

The feel of his mouth was extraordinary, at once entreating and demanding, tender and rough, soft and firm. By the time he pulled back, her brain was so rattled all she could do was say the first thing that popped into her head. "I thought you didn't like me."

He nuzzled the curve where her neck joined her shoulder. "Oh, I like you very much."

"You think I took advantage of your father."

"I don't think that at all."

"Since when?"

* * *

Only on His Terms is part of
The Accidental Heirs duet:
First they find their fortunes, then they find love.

Dear Reader,

I confess I'm a bit of a TV addict. And also a major insomniac. Put the two conditions together and you have someone who discovers all kinds of interesting stuff on the higher cable channels at three o'clock in the morning. Such was the case with a British show called *Heir Hunters*, which I found fascinating. The members of a probate law firm search for long-lost relatives of people who've passed away without a will or who had no known heirs. Often the heirs they found had no idea they were the recipients of— sometimes significant—estates.

This kind of situation is just perfect for that writer question "What if...?"

What if someone going about his or her normal daily life was suddenly informed s/he was the heir/ ess to a fortune? What if, say, a waitress working her way through college discovered her former elderly neighbor, a retired TV repairman and stand-in grandfather, was in fact a twenty-first century Howard Hughes who left her his entire estate when he died? And what if he left behind an estranged son who suspected her of conning his father out of that fortune for nefarious reasons? Talk about an opportunity for sparks to fly!

Gracie and Harrison's story is the first in a series of such what-if situations. I hope you have fun reading about them. And I hope you'll check back for the rest of the Accidental Heirs books. Because I'm having a lot of fun writing them.

Happy reading,

Elizabeth

ONLY ON HIS TERMS

ELIZABETH BEVARLY

HARLEQUIN® DESIRE

Recycling programs
for this product may
not exist in your area.

ISBN-13: 978-0-373-73413-9

Only on His Terms

Printed in U.S.A.

Elizabeth Bevarly is a *New York Times* bestselling and award-winning author of more than seventy novels and novellas. Her books have been translated into two dozen languages and published in three dozen countries, and she hopes to someday be as well traveled herself. An honors graduate of the University of Louisville, she has called home places as diverse as San Juan, Puerto Rico and Haddonfield, New Jersey, but now writes full-time in her native Kentucky, usually on a futon between two cats. She loves reading, movies, British and Canadian TV shows, and fiddling with soup recipes. Visit her on the web at elizabethbevarly.com, follow her on Twitter or send her a friend request on Facebook.

Books by Elizabeth Bevarly

Harlequin Desire

Taming the Prince
Taming the Beastly M.D.
Married to His Business
The Billionaire Gets His Way

The Accidental Heirs

Only on His Terms

Visit the Author Profile page at Harlequin.com or elizabethbevarly.com for more titles.

For Wanda Ottewell.
With many, many thanks
and even more fond memories.

Prologue

Gracie Sumner came from a long line of waitresses. Her mother worked for a popular chain restaurant for three decades, and her grandmother manned the counter of a gleaming silver diner on the Great White Way. The tradition went all the way back to her great-great-great-grandmother, in fact, who welcomed westward-ho train passengers to a Denver saloon. Gracie may have brought a bit more prestige to the family trade by finding work in a four-star, Zagat-approved bistro, but the instinct and artistry of waitressing was pretty much encoded on her DNA, the same way her tawny hair and brown eyes were.

And that instinct was how she knew there was something more to the silver-haired gentleman seated at table fifteen of Seattle's Café Destiné than a desire to sample the pot-au-feu.

He had come in at the end of the lunch shift and asked specifically to be seated in her area, then engaged her in conversation in a way that made her feel as if he already knew her. But neither he nor the name on the credit card he placed atop his check—Bennett Tarrant—was familiar. That wasn't surprising, however, since judging by his bespoke suit and platinum card, he was clearly a man of means. Unlike Gracie, who was struggling to pay her way through college, and who, at twenty-six, still had three semesters left before earning her BA in early childhood education.

"Here you go, Mr. Tarrant," she said as she placed the server book back on the table. "I hope you'll visit Café Destiné again soon."

"Actually, Miss Sumner, there's a reason why I came here today."

Her gaze flew to his. Although she always introduced herself as Gracie to her customers, she never gave out her last name. Warily, she replied, "The pot-au-feu. Yes, it's the most popular item on our menu."

"And it was delicious," Mr. Tarrant assured her. "But I really came in to see you on behalf of a client. I inquired for you at your apartment first, and your landlady told me where you work."

Good old Mrs. Mancini. Gracie could always count on her to guard absolutely no one's privacy.

Mr. Tarrant withdrew a silver case from inside his suit jacket and handed her a business card. Tarrant, Fiver & Twigg, it read, and there was a New York City address. Bennett Tarrant's title was President and Senior Probate Researcher. Which told Gracie all of nothing.

She looked at him again. "I'm sorry, but I don't understand. What's a probate researcher?"

"I'm an attorney. My firm is one of several appointed by the State of New York when someone passes away without a will, or when a beneficiary named in someone's will can't be found. In such circumstances, we locate the rightful heirs."

Gracie's confusion deepened. "I still don't understand. My mother died in Cincinnati, and her estate was settled years ago."

Not that there had been much to settle. Marian Sumner had left Gracie just enough to cover four months' rent and modestly furnish a one-bedroom apartment. Still, she had been grateful for even that.

"It's not your mother's estate my firm was appointed to research," Mr. Tarrant said. "Did you know a man by the name of Harrison Sage?"

Gracie shook her head. "I'm afraid not."

"How about Harry Sagalowsky?"

"Oh, sure, I knew Harry. His apartment was across from mine when I lived in Cincinnati. He was such a nice man."

For a moment, she was overrun by warm memories. Harry had been living in the other apartment on the top floor of the renovated Victorian when Gracie moved in after her mother's death. They had become instant friends—he filled the role of the grandfather she never had, and she was the granddaughter he never had. She introduced him to J. K. Rowling and Bruno Mars and taught him how to crush the competition in *Call of Duty*. He turned her on to Patricia Highsmith and Miles Davis and taught her how to fox-trot at the Moondrop Ballroom.

She sobered. "He died two years ago. Even though I haven't lived in Cincinnati for a while now, when I come home from work, I still halfway expect him to open his front door and tell me how he just got *The African Queen* from Netflix or how he made too much chili for one person." Her voice trailed off. "I just miss him. A lot."

Mr. Tarrant smiled gently. "Mr. Sagalowsky thought very highly of you, too. He remembered you in his will, which was just recently settled."

Gracie smiled at that. Although Harry's apartment had been crowded with stuff that was both eclectic and eccentric, nothing could have been worth much. After his death, she helped their landlord pack it all up, but no one ever came to claim it—Harry had never spoken of any family, so she'd had no idea whom to contact. Their landlord finally decided to toss it all, but Gracie offered to rent a storage unit for it instead. It had meant tightening her belt even more, but she hadn't been able to stand the thought of Harry's things rotting in a dump. She was still paying for the unit back in Cincinnati. She brightened. Maybe Mr. Tarrant could help her get it all into the hands of Harry's next of kin.

"I'm afraid it took me a while to find you," he continued.

She stiffened. "Yeah, I kind of left Cincinnati on a whim about a year and a half ago."

"Without leaving a forwarding address?"

"I, um, had a bad breakup with a guy. It seemed like a good time to start fresh. My mom and Harry were gone, and most of my friends from high school moved after graduation. I didn't really have many ties there anymore."

Mr. Tarrant nodded, but she got the feeling he wasn't too familiar with bad romance. "If you have some time today," he said, "we can discuss Mr. Sagalowsky's estate and the changes it will mean for you."

Gracie almost laughed at that. He made Harry sound like some batty Howard Hughes, squirreling away a fortune while he wore tissue boxes for shoes.

"There's a coffee shop up the street," she said. "Mimi's Mocha Java. I can meet you there in about twenty minutes."

"Perfect," Mr. Tarrant told her. "We have a lot to talk about."

One

As Gracie climbed out of Mr. Tarrant's Jaguar coupe in the driveway of the house Harry had abandoned fifteen years ago—the house that now belonged to her—she told herself not to worry, that the place couldn't possibly be as bad as it seemed. Why, the weathered clapboard was actually kind of quaint. And the scattered pea-gravel drive was kind of adorable. So what if the size of the place wasn't what she'd been expecting? So what if the, ah, overabundant landscaping was going to require a massive amount of work? The house was fine. Just fine. She had no reason to feel apprehensive about being its new owner. The place was…charming. Yeah, that was it. Absolutely…charming.

In a waterfront, Long Island, multi-multi-multi-million-dollar kind of way. Holy cow, Harry's old house could host the United Arab Emirates and still have room left over for Luxembourg.

In spite of the serene ocean that sparkled beyond the house and the salty June breeze that caressed her face, she felt herself growing light-headed again—a not unfamiliar sensation since meeting Mr. Tarrant last week. After all, their encounter at Mimi's Mocha Java had culminated in Gracie sitting with her head between her knees, breathing in and out of a paper bag with the phrase Coffee, Chocolate, Men—Some Things are Better Rich printed on it. To his credit, Mr. Tarrant hadn't batted an eye. He'd just patted her gently on the back and told her everything was going to be fine, and the fact that she'd just inherited fourteen billion—yes, *billion,* with a *b*—dollars was nothing to have a panic attack about.

Hah. Easy for him to say. He probably knew what to do with fourteen billion dollars. Other than have a panic attack over it.

Now that they were here, he seemed to sense her trepidation—probably because of the way her breathing was starting to turn into hyperventilation again—because he looped his arm gently through hers. "We shouldn't keep Mrs. Sage and her son and their attorneys—or Mr. Sage's colleagues and their attorneys—waiting. I'm sure they're all as anxious to get the formalities out of the way as you are."

Anxious. Right. That was one word for it, Gracie thought. Had the situation been reversed, had she been the one to discover that her long-estranged husband or father, a titan of twentieth-century commerce, had spent his final years posing as a retired TV repairman in the blue-collar Cincinnati neighborhood where he grew up, then befriended a stranger to whom he had left nearly everything, she supposed she'd be a tad anxious, too. She just hoped there weren't other words for what Vivian Sage and her son, Harrison III, might be. Like *furious*. Or *vindictive*. Or *homicidal*.

At least she was dressed for the occasion. Not homicide, of course, but for the formal reading of Harry's will. Even though Harry's will had already been read a few times, mostly in court, because it had been contested and appealed by just about everyone he'd known in life. This time would be the last, Mr. Tarrant had promised, and this time it was for Gracie. She looked her very best, if she did say so herself, wearing the nicest of the vintage outfits that she loved—a beige, sixties-era suit with pencil skirt and cropped jacket that would have looked right at home on Jackie Kennedy. She'd even taken care to put on some makeup and fix her hair, managing a fairly convincing French twist from which just a few errant strands had escaped.

She and Mr. Tarrant moved forward, toward a surprisingly modest front porch. As he rapped the worn knocker, Gracie could almost convince herself she was visiting any number of normal suburban homes. But the humbleness ended once the door was opened by a liveried butler, and she looked beyond him into the house. The entryway alone was larger than her apartment back in Seattle, and it was crowded with period antiques, authentic hand-knotted Persian rugs and original works of art.

She began to take a step backward, but Mr. Tarrant nudged her forward again. He announced their names to the butler, who led them through the foyer and down a hall to the left, then another hall to the right, until they were standing in the entryway of a cavernous library. Gracie knew it was a library because three walls were virtually covered by floor-to-ceiling bookcases filled with exquisite leather-bound collectors' editions. They matched nicely the exquisite leather-bound furnishings. And there were floor-to-ceiling windows that looked out onto the gleaming water. She might as well have fallen through the looking glass, so grand and foreign was this world to her.

Her breathing settled some when she realized the room was full of people, since that would make it easier for her to be invisible. Mr. Tarrant had cautioned her that there would be a veritable army of attorneys present, along with their clients—Harry's former business associates and family members. It had come as no small surprise to hear that Harry had left behind a widow and two ex-wives, along with three daughters by the exes and a solitary son by his last wife. Gracie had no idea how to tell one person from another, though, since everyone was dressed alike—the men in suits and the women in more suits and a couple of sedate dresses—and they represented a variety of age groups.

One of those suited men hailed Mr. Tarrant from the other side of the room, and after ensuring that Gracie would be all right for a few minutes without him, he strode in that direction. So she took a few steps into the fray, relieved to be able to do it on her own.

See? she said to herself. This wasn't so bad. It was just like working a wedding-rehearsal dinner at Café Destiné for some wealthy Seattle bride and groom. Except that she would be in the background at one of those events, not front and center, which would be happening here all too soon. Not to mention that, at a rehearsal dinner, she'd be sharing 18 percent of a final tab worth a couple of thousand dollars with two or three other waiters, and here, she would be receiving 100 percent of almost everything.

Fourteen billion—yes, *billion* with a *b*—dollars.

She felt her panic advancing again, until a gentle voice murmured from behind her, "How can you tell the difference between a bunch of high-powered suits and a pack of bloodthirsty jackals?"

She spun around to find herself gazing up—and up and up some more—into a pair of the most beautiful blue eyes she had ever seen. The rest of the man's face was every bit as appealing, with straight ebony brows, an aristocratic nose, a sculpted jaw and lips that were just this side of full. Not to mention a strand of black hair that tumbled rebelliously over his forehead in a way that made him look as if he'd just sauntered out of a fabulous forties film.

She took a quick inventory of the rest of him, pretending she didn't notice how he was doing the same to her. He had broad shoulders, a slim waist and the merest scent of something smoky and vaguely indecent. Gracie couldn't have identified a current fashion label if her life depended on it, but it was a safe bet that his charcoal pinstripes had been designed by whoever had the most expensive one. He looked like one of the high-powered suits in the riddle he'd just posed and nothing like a bloodthirsty jackal. She couldn't wait to hear the answer.

"I don't know," she said. "How can you tell the difference?"

He grinned, something that made him downright dazzling. Gracie did her best not to swoon.

In a voice tinted with merriment, he said, "You can't."

She chuckled, and the tension that had wrapped her so tightly for the last week began to ease for the first time. For that, more than anything, she was grateful to the man. Not that she didn't appreciate his other, ah, attributes, too. A lot.

"But you're one of those suits," she objected.

"Only because professional dictates say I have to be."

As if to illustrate his reluctance, he tugged his necktie loose enough to unbutton the top button of his shirt. In a way, he reminded her of Harry, someone who knew there was more to life than appearances, and there were better ways to spend time than currying the favor of others.

"Would you like some coffee?" he asked. "There's an urn in the corner. And some cookies or something, too, I think."

She shook her head. "No, thanks. I'm good." She didn't add that the addition of even a drop of caffeine or a grain of sugar to her system would turn her jitters into a seismic event. "But if you'd like some—" She started to tell him she'd be right back with a cup and a plate, so automatically did her waitress response come out.

But he offered no indication that he expected her to get it for him. "No, I've had my quota for the day, too."

The conversation seemed ready to stall, and Gracie was desperate to hold on to the only friend she was likely to make today. As a result, she blurted out the first thing that popped into her head. "So...this house. This room. This view. Is this place gorgeous or what?"

Her question seemed to stump him. He glanced

around the library as if he were seeing it for the first time, but he didn't seem nearly as impressed as she. "It's all right, I guess. The room's a little formal for my taste, and the view's a little boring, but…"

It was a rare individual who wouldn't covet a house as grand as this, Gracie thought. Although she had no intention of keeping it or much of anything else Harry had left her, since fourteen billion—yes, *billion* with a *b*—dollars was way too much money for a single individual to have, she still felt a keen appreciation for its beauty.

"Well, what kind of place do you call home?" she asked.

Without hesitation, he told her, "Bright lights, big city. I've lived in Manhattan since I started college, and I'm never leaving."

His enthusiasm for the fast-paced setting didn't seem to fit with how he'd reminded her of Harry earlier. But she tried to sound convincing when she said, "Oh. Okay."

She must not have done a very good job, though, because he said, "You sound surprised."

"I guess I am, kind of."

"Why?" He suddenly seemed a little defensive.

She shrugged. "Maybe because I was just thinking how you remind me of someone I used to know, and he wasn't a bright-lights, big-city kind of guy at all."

At least, he hadn't been when Gracie knew him. But Harry's life before that? Who knew? Nothing she'd discovered about him in the past week had seemed true to the man she'd called her friend for years.

Her new friend's wariness seemed to increase. "Old boyfriend?"

"Well, old, anyway," Gracie said with a smile. "More like a grandfather, though."

He relaxed visibly, but still looked sweetly abashed. "You know, the last thing a guy wants to hear when he's trying to impress a beautiful woman he's just met is how he reminds her of her grandfather."

He thought she was beautiful? Was he trying to impress her? And was he actually admitting it? Did he know how one of her turn-ons, coming in second after a bewitching smile, was men who spoke frankly and honestly? Especially because she'd known so few of them. Really, none other than Harry.

"I, uh…" she stammered. "I mean, um, ah…"

He seemed to take great pleasure in having rendered her speechless. Not arrogantly so, but as if he were simply delighted by his success. "So you're not a big-city type yourself?"

Grateful for the change of subject—and something she could respond to with actual words—she shook her head. "Not at all. I mean, I've lived in big cities all my life, but never in the city proper. I've always been a suburban girl."

Even though she'd never known her father and had lived in an apartment growing up, her life had been no different from her friends' who'd lived in houses with yards and a two-parents-and-siblings family unit. Her mother had been active at her school and the leader of her Brownie troop. And even with her meager income, Marian Sumner had somehow always had enough for summer vacations and piano and gymnastics lessons. As a girl, Gracie had spent summers playing in the park, autumns jumping into leaf piles, winters building snowmen and springs riding her bike. Completely unremarkable. Totally suburban.

Her new friend considered her again, but this time, he seemed to be taking in something other than her physical appearance. "At first, I was thinking you seem like the city type, too. The suit is a little retro, but you'd still be right at home in the East Village or Williamsburg. Now, though…"

His voice trailed off before he completed his analysis, and he studied Gracie in the most interesting—and interested—way. Heat pooled in her midsection, spiraling outward, until every cell she possessed felt as if it was going to catch fire. The entire room seemed to go silent for an interminable moment, as if everyone else had disappeared, and it was just the two of them alone in the universe. She'd never experienced anything like it before. It was…unsettling. But nice.

"Now?" she echoed, hoping to spur his response and end the curious spell. The word came out so quietly, however, and he still seemed so lost in thought, that she wondered if he'd even heard her.

He shook his head almost imperceptibly, as if he were trying to physically dispel the thoughts from his brain. "Now I think maybe you do seem like the wholesome girl next door."

This time, it was Gracie's turn to look abashed. "You know, the last thing a girl wants to hear when she's trying to impress a beautiful man she's just met is how she reminds him of a glass of milk."

That, finally, seemed to break the weird enchantment. Both of them laughed lightly, but she suspected it was as much due to relief that the tension had evaporated as it was to finding humor in the remark.

"Do you have to go back to work after this thing?" he asked. "Or would you maybe be free for a late lunch?"

In spite of the banter they'd been sharing, the invitation came out of nowhere and caught Gracie off-guard. A million questions cartwheeled through her brain, and she had no idea how to respond to any of them. How had her morning gone from foreboding to flirtatious? Where had this guy come from? How could she like him so much after only knowing him a matter of moments? And how on earth was she supposed to accept an invitation to lunch with him when her entire life was about to explode in a way that was nothing short of atomic?

She tried to reply with something that made sense, but all that came out was "Lunch…? I…? Work…?"

He was clearly enjoying how much he continued to keep her off-kilter. "Yeah, lunch. Yeah, you. As for your work, which firm do you work for?" He glanced around the room. "Maybe I can pull some strings for you. I've known most of these people all my life. A couple of them owe me favors."

"Firm?" she echoed, the single word all she could manage in her growing confusion.

"Which law firm, representing which one of my father's interests?" For the first time since they began chatting, he sobered. "Not that they're my father's interests anymore. Not since that trashy, scheming, manipulative gold digger got her hooks into him. Not that my mother and I are going down without a fight."

It dawned on Gracie then—dawned like a two-by-four to the back of her head—that the man to whom she had been speaking so warmly wasn't one of the many attorneys who were here representing Harry's former colleagues. Nor was he one of those colleagues. It was Harry's son, Harrison Sage III. The man who had assumed he would, along with his mother, inherit the bulk of his father's fortune. The one whom Gracie had prevented from doing just that. The one she had earlier been thinking might be furious, vindictive and homicidal.

Then his other remark hit her. The part about the trashy, scheming, manipulative gold digger. That was what he thought she was? Her? The woman whose idea of stilettos was a kitten heel? The woman who preferred her hemlines below the knee? The woman who'd nearly blinded herself that morning with a mascara wand? The woman who intended to give away nearly every nickel of the fourteen billion—yes *billion* with a *b*—dollars with which Harry had entrusted her?

Because even without Mr. Tarrant's having told her about Harry's wish that she give away the bulk of his fortune to make the world a better place, Gracie would have done just that. She didn't want the responsibility that came with so much money. She didn't want the notoriety. She didn't want the pandemonium. She didn't want the terror.

Maybe she'd been struggling to make ends meet before last week, but she had been making them meet. And she'd been happy with her life in Seattle. She had fun friends. She had a cute apartment. She was gainfully employed. She was working toward her degree. She'd had hope for the future in general and a sunny outlook for any given day. Since finding out about her inheritance, however, she'd awoken every morning with a nervous stomach, and had only been able to sleep every night with a pill. In between those times, she'd been jumpy, withdrawn and scared.

Most people would probably think she was nuts, but Gracie didn't want to be a billionaire. She didn't even want to be a millionaire. She wanted to have enough so that she could make it through life without worrying, but not so much that she spent the rest of her life worrying. Did that make sense? To her, it did. To Harry's son, however…

She searched for words that would explain everything to Harrison Sage III quickly enough that he wouldn't have time to believe she was any of the things he'd just called her. But there was still so much of it she didn't understand herself. How could she explain it to him when even she couldn't make sense of it?

"I, um, that is…" she began. She inhaled a deep breath and released it, and then shifted her weight nervously from one foot to the other. She forced a smile she was sure looked as contrived as it felt and tried again. "Actually, I mean… The thing is…"

Gah. At this rate, she would be seeing Harry in the afterlife before she was able to make a complete sentence. *Just spit it out,* she told herself. But all she finally ended up saying was "Um, actually, I don't have to go back to work after this."

Well, it was a start. Not to mention the truth. *Go, Gracie!*

Immediately, Harrison Sage's expression cleared. "Excellent," he said. "Do you like Thai? Because there's this great place on West Forty-Sixth that just opened. You'll love it."

"I do like Thai," she said. Still being honest. *Forward, Gracie*, she told herself. *Move forward.*

"Excellent," he said, treating her again to that bewitching smile. "I'm Harrison, by the way," he added. "Harrison Sage. If you hadn't already figured that out."

Gracie bit back a strangled sound. "Yeah, I kinda did."

"And you are?"

It was all she could do not to reply, "I'm the trashy, scheming, manipulative gold digger. Nice to meet you."

"I'm—I'm Gracie," she said instead.

She was hoping the name was common enough that he wouldn't make the connection to the woman he probably hated with the burning passion of a thousand fiery suns. But she was pretty sure he did make the connection. She could tell by the way his expression went stony, by the way his eyes went flinty, by the way his jaw went clinchy...

And by the way the temperature in the room seemed to drop about fourteen billion—yes *billion* with a *b*—degrees.

Two

Harrison Sage told himself he must have misheard her. Maybe she hadn't said her name was Gracie. Maybe she'd said her name was Stacy. Or Tracy. Or even Maisey. Because Gracie was a nickname for Grace. And Grace was the name of the woman who had used her sexual wiles to seduce and manipulate a fragile old man into changing his will to leave her with nearly every nickel he had.

This was that woman? he thought, taking her in again. He'd been expecting a loudmouthed, garishly painted, platinum blonde in a short skirt, tight sweater and mile-high heels. One who had big hair, long legs and absolutely enormous—

Well. He just hadn't expected her to look like something out of a fairy tale. But that was exactly the impression he'd formed of this woman when she first walked into the room. That she was some fey, other-worldly sylph completely out of her element in this den of trolls. She was slight and wispy, and if she was wearing any makeup, he sure couldn't see it. Stray tendrils of hair, the color of a golden autumn sunset, had escaped their twist, as if all it would take was a breath of sorcery to make the entire mass tumble free.

And when had he become such a raging poet? he asked himself. Golden autumn sunset? Breath of sorcery? What the hell kind of thoughts were those to have about a woman who had robbed his family of their rightful legacy? What the hell kind of thoughts were those for a man to have, period? Where the hell had his testosterone got to?

On the other hand, he was beginning to see how his father had been taken in by her. Obviously, she was the kind of grifter who got better results as a vestal virgin than a blonde bombshell. Harrison had almost fallen into her trap himself.

It didn't matter *how* she'd conned his father. What mattered was that she'd swindled one of the last century's most savvy businessmen and convinced him to turn his back on everyone and everything he'd loved in life. Well, as far as his father *could* have loved anyone or anything—other than his fortune, his commercial holdings and his social standing. But then, what else was there to love? Money, power and position were the only things a person could count on. Or, at least, they had been, before everything went to hell, thanks to this, this...

Harrison took a step backward, and met Grace Sumner's gaze coolly. "*You're* the trashy, scheming, manipulative gold digger?" he asked. Then, because something in her expression looked genuinely wounded by the comment—wow, she really was good—he tempered it by adding, "I thought you'd be taller."

She mustered a smile he would have sworn was filled with anxiety if he hadn't known she was a woman who made her way in the world by conning people. "Well, I guess zero out of five isn't bad."

Harrison opened his mouth to say something else, but Bennett Tarrant—another thorn in the Sage family's side for the last two years—appeared next to Gracie, as if conjured by one of her magic spells.

"I see you've met Mr. Sage," he said unnecessarily.

"Yep," Grace said, her gaze never leaving Harrison's.

Tarrant turned to Harrison. "And I see you've met Miss Sumner."

"Yep," Harrison said, his gaze never leaving Grace's.

The silence that ensued was thick enough to hack with a meat cleaver. Until Tarrant said, "We should head for our seats. We'll be starting shortly."

Instead of doing as Tarrant instructed, Harrison found it impossible to move his feet—or remove his gaze from Grace Sumner. Damn. She really was some kind of enchantress.

In an effort to make himself move away, he reminded himself of everything he and his mother had been through since his father's disappearance fifteen years ago. And he reminded himself how his mother would be left with nothing, thanks to this woman who had, by sheer, dumb luck, stumbled onto an opportunity to bleed the last drop out of a rich, feeble-minded old man.

Fifteen years ago—half a lifetime—Harrison had

gone down to breakfast to find his parents seated, as they always were, at a dining-room table capable of seating twenty-two people. But instead of sitting side by side, they sat at each end, as far apart as possible. As usual, his father had had his nose buried in the *Wall Street Journal* while his mother had been flipping through the pages of a program for Milan Fashion Week. Or maybe Paris Fashion Week. Or London Fashion Week. Or, hell, Lickspittle, Idaho, Fashion Week for all he knew. So he'd taken his regular place at the table midway between them, ensuring that none of them was close enough to speak to the others. It was, after all, a Sage family tradition to not speak to each other.

They'd eaten in silence until their butler entered with his daily reminder that his father's car had arrived to take him to work, his mother's car had arrived to take her shopping and Harrison's car had arrived to take him to school. All three Sages had then risen and made their way to their destinations, none saying a word of farewell—just as they had every morning. Had Harrison realized then that that would be the last time he ever saw his father, he might have...

What? he asked himself. Told him to have a nice day? Given him a hug? Said, "I love you"? He wasn't sure he'd even known how to do any of those things when he was fifteen. He wasn't sure he knew how to do any of them now. But he might at least have told his father...something.

He tamped down a wave of irritation. He just wished he and his father had talked more. Or at all. But that was kind of hard to do when the father spent 90 percent of his time at work and the son spent 90 percent of his time in trouble. Because Harrison remembered something else about that day. The night before his father took off, Harrison had come home in the backseat of a squad car, because he'd been caught helping himself to a couple of porno magazines and a bottle of malt liquor at a midtown bodega.

Five months after his father's disappearance had come the news from one of the family's attorneys that he had been found, but that he had no intention of coming home just yet. Oh, he would stay in touch with one of his attorneys and a couple of business associates, to make sure the running of Sage Holdings, Inc. continued at its usual pace and to keep himself from being declared legally dead. But he wouldn't return to his work life—or his home life—anytime soon. To those few with whom he stayed in contact he paid a bundle to never reveal his whereabouts. He'd come back when he felt like it, he said. And then he never came back at all.

Harrison looked at Grace Sumner again, at the deceptively beautiful face and the limitless dark eyes. Maybe two judges had decided she was entitled to the personal fortune his father had left behind. But there was no way Harrison was going down without a fight. He would prove once and for all, unequivocally, that she wasn't entitled to a cent. He'd been so sure the appeals court would side with the family that he hadn't felt it necessary to play his full hand. Until now. And now...

Soon everyone would know that the last thing Grace Sumner was was a fey, unearthly creature. In fact, she was right at home in this den of trolls.

Gracie wanted very much to say something to Harry's son before leaving with Mr. Tarrant. But his expression had gone so chilly, she feared anything she offered by way of an explanation or condolences would go unheard. Still, she couldn't just walk away. The man had lost his father—twice—and had no chance to make amends at this point. His family's life had been turned upside down because of Harry's last wishes and what he'd asked her to do with his fortune. She supposed she couldn't blame Harrison III for the cool reception.

Nevertheless, she braved a small smile and told him, "I doubt you'll believe me, but it *was* nice to meet you, Mr. Sage. I'm so sorry about your father. He was the kindest, most decent man I ever met."

Without giving him a chance to respond, she turned to follow Mr. Tarrant to the other side of the room, where chairs had been set up for everyone affected by Harry's will. They were arranged in two arcs that faced each other, with a big-screen TV on one side. She seated herself between Mr. Tarrant and two attorneys from his firm, almost as if the three of them were circling the wagons to protect her.

Gus Fiver, the second in command at Tarrant, Fiver & Twigg, looked to be in his midthirties and was as fair and amiable as Harrison Sage was dark and moody—though Gus's pinstripes looked to be every bit as expensive. Renny Twigg, whom Mr. Tarrant had introduced as one of their associates—her father was the Twigg in the company's name—was closer in age to Gracie's twenty-six. Renny was a petite brunette who didn't seem quite as comfortable in her own pinstripes. Even with her tidy chignon and perfectly manicured hands, she looked like the kind of woman who would be happier working outdoors, preferably at a job that involved wearing flannel.

Everyone else in the room was either connected to Harry in some way or an attorney representing someone's interests. Seated directly across from Gracie—naturally—were Harry's surviving family members and their attorneys. In addition to Harrison Sage III, there was his mother and Harry's widow, Vivian Sage, not to mention a veritable stable of ex-wives and mistresses and a half-dozen additional children—three of whom were even legitimate. As far as professional interests went, Harry had had conglomerates and corporations by the boatload. Add them together, and it totaled a financial legacy of epic proportion. Nearly all of what hadn't gone back to the businesses was now legally Gracie's. Harry had left a little to a handful of other people, but the rest of his fortune—every brick, byte and buck—had gone to her.

Oh, where was a paper bag for hyperventilating into when she needed it?

Once everyone was seated and silent, Bennett Tarrant rose to address the crowd. "Thank you all for coming. This meeting is just a formality, since Mr. Sage's estate has been settled by the court, and—"

"Settled doesn't mean the ruling can't be appealed," Harrison Sage interrupted, his voice booming enough to make Gracie flinch. "And we plan to file within the next two weeks."

"I can't imagine how that's necessary," Mr. Tarrant said. "An appeal has already supported the court's initial ruling in Miss Sumner's favor. Unless some new information comes to light, any additional appeal will only uphold those rulings."

Harrison opened his mouth to say more, but his attorney, a man of Mr. Tarrant's age and demeanor, placed a hand lightly on his arm to halt him. "New information will come to light," the man said.

Mr. Tarrant looked in no way concerned. "Mr. Landis, it has been twice determined that Harrison Sage, Jr., was of sound mind and body when he left the bulk of his personal estate to Grace Sumner. Another appeal would be—"

"Actually, we'll disprove that this time," Mr. Landis stated unequivocally. "And we will prove that not only did Grace Sumner exert undue influence over Mr. Sage of a sexual nature, but that—"

"What?" This time Gracie was the one to interrupt.

Mr. Landis ignored her, but she could practically feel the heat of Harrison Sage's gaze.

Mr. Landis continued, "We'll prove that not only did Grace Sumner exert undue influence over Mr. Sage of a sexual nature, but that he contracted a sexually transmitted disease from her which rendered him mentally incapacitated."

"What?" Gracie erupted even more loudly.

She started to rise from her chair, but Gus Fiver gently covered her shoulder with his hand, willing her to ignore the allegation. With much reluctance, Gracie made herself relax. But if looks could kill, the one she shot Harrison Sage would have rendered him a pile of ash.

Especially after his attorney concluded, "She used sex to seduce and further incapacitate an already fragile old man, and then took advantage of his diminished state to convince him to leave his money and assets to her. We're hiring a private investigator to gather the necessary evidence, since this is something that has only recently come to light."

"I see," Mr. Tarrant replied. "Or perhaps it's something you've pulled out of thin air in a vain last-ditch effort."

Unbelievable, Gracie thought. Even if she'd known Harry was worth a bundle, she never would have taken advantage of him. And she certainly wouldn't have used her alleged *sexual wiles*, since she didn't even have *a* sexual wile, never mind sexual *wiles*, plural. True friendship was worth way more than money and was a lot harder to find. And incapacitated? Diminished? Harry? Please. He'd been full of piss and vinegar until the minute that damned aneurysm brought him down.

Mr. Tarrant met the other attorney's gaze levelly. "Harrison Sage, Jr. changed his will in person, in the office of his attorneys, two of whom are seated in this room. And he presented to them not only a document from his physician stating his excellent health, both mental and physical, but his physician was also present to bear witness in that office. Your father's intent was crystal clear. He wished for Grace Sumner to inherit the bulk of his personal estate. Two judges have agreed. Therefore Miss Sumner *does* inherit the bulk of his personal estate.

"Now then," he continued, "on the day he amended his will for the last time, Mr. Sage also made a video at his attorneys' office that he wanted Miss Sumner and his family and associates, along with their representatives, to view. Renny, do you mind?"

Renny Twigg aimed a remote at the TV. A second later, Harry's face appeared on the screen, and Gracie's stomach dropped. He looked nothing like the Harry she remembered. He was wearing a suit and tie not unlike the other power suits in the room, a garment completely at odds with the wrinkled khakis and sweatshirts he'd always worn in Cincinnati. His normally untidy hair had been cut and styled by a pro. His expression was stern, and his eyes were flinty. He looked like a billion-aire corporate mogul—humorless, ruthless and mean. Then he smiled his Santa Claus smile and winked, and she knew this was indeed the Harry she had known and loved. Suddenly, she felt much better.

"Hey there, Gracie," he said in the same playful voice with which he'd always greeted her. "I'm sorry we're meeting like this, kiddo, because it means I'm dead."

Unbidden tears pricked Gracie's eyes. She really did miss Harry. He was the best friend she'd ever had. Without thinking, she murmured, "Hi, Harry."

Every eye in the room fell upon her, but Gracie didn't care. Let them think she was a lunatic, talking to someone on a TV screen. In that moment, it felt as if Harry were right there with her. And it had been a long time since she'd been able to talk to him.

"And if you're watching this," he continued, "it also means you know the truth about who I really am, and that you're having to share a room with members of my original tribe. I know from experience what a pain in the ass that can be, so I'll keep this as brief as I can. Here's the deal, kiddo. I hope it didn't scare the hell out of you when you heard how much I left you. I'm sorry I never told you the truth about myself when I was alive. But by the time I met you, I was way more Harry Sagalowsky than I was Harrison Sage, so I wasn't re-ally lying. You wouldn't have liked Harrison, anyway. He was a prick."

At this, Gracie laughed out loud. It was just such a Harry thing to say. When she felt eyes on her again, she bit her lip to stifle any further inappropriate outbursts. Inappropriate to those in the room, anyway. Harry wouldn't have minded her reaction at all.

He continued, "That's why I wanted to stop being Harrison. One day, I realized just how far I'd gotten from my roots, and how much of myself I'd lost along the way. People love rags-to-riches stories like mine, but those stories never mention all the sacrifices you have to make while you're clawing for those riches, and how a lot of those sacrifices are of your morals, your ethics and your character."

Gracie sobered at that. She'd never heard Harry sound so serious. He grew more so as he described how, by the time he'd left his old life, he'd become little more than a figurehead for his companies, and how unhappy his home life had become, and how all he'd wanted was to escape. So he left his work, his family and his "big-ass Long Island estate," returned to the surname his ancestors had changed generations ago and moved back to the blue-collar neighborhood in Cincinnati where he grew up.

At this, Gracie glanced across the room at Vivian and Harrison and saw them looking at the television with identical expressions—a mixture of annoyance, confusion and something else she couldn't identify. She tried to be sympathetic. She couldn't imagine what it must be like for them, being ignored by their husband and father for fifteen years, and then being disinherited by him. She supposed they were justified in some of their feelings toward Harry.

But maybe they should take a minute to wonder

why Harry had done this. He hadn't been the kind of man to turn his back on people, unless those people had given him a reason to do it.

Harry spoke from the video again, bringing Gracie's attention back around. "Vivian and Harrison, this part is for you. Billions of dollars is way too much for anyone to have. Gracie Sumner is the kind of person who will understand what an awesome responsibility that much money is, and she'll do the right thing by it. She won't keep it for herself. I know her. She'll get rid of it as quickly as she can, and she'll make sure it gets into the hands of people who need it."

At this, Gracie braved another look across the room. Vivian Sage, her hair silver, her suit gold, her fingers and wrists bedecked in gemstones of every color, looked like she wanted to cry. Harrison, however, was staring right at Gracie. But his expression was unreadable. He could have been wondering where to eat lunch later or pondering where to hide her body. She hadn't a clue.

Thankfully, Harry's mention of her name gave her a reason to look back at the TV. "Gracie, this part's for you. I could have given my money to worthy causes myself and saved you a lot of trouble. But being a better person than I am, you'll know better than I would what to do with all my filthy lucre. But listen, kiddo. This last part is really important. Keep some of the money for yourself. I mean it. Buy yourself one of those ridiculous little cars you like. Or a house on the water. Go to Spain like you said you wanted to. Something. You promise?"

Again, Gracie felt every gaze in the room arc toward her. She had no idea what to say. It just felt wrong to take Harry's money, even a modest sum. After that first meeting with Mr. Tarrant, Gracie had gone home and headed straight for Google. In every article she'd read about Harrison Sage, Jr., he'd been defined by his wealth. "Billionaire Harrison Sage, Jr.," he'd invariably been called. Even after his disappearance, when the word *recluse* had been added to his descriptions, it had still always been preceded by the word *billionaire*. In his old life, Harry had been, first and foremost, rich. Anything else had been incidental. Gracie didn't want to be one of the people who saw only dollar signs in conjunction with his name, and she didn't want to be one of the ones who took from him. Especially after he'd given so much to her.

"Promise me, Gracie," he said again from the big screen, obviously having known she would hesitate.

"Okay, Harry," she replied softly. "I promise."

"That's my girl," Harry said with another wink.

He said his farewells, and then the TV screen went dark. Again, Gracie felt tears threatening. Hastily, she fished a handkerchief out of her purse and pressed it first to one eye, then the other.

Across the room, Harrison Sage began a slow clap. "Oh, well done, Ms. Sumner," he said. "Definitely an award-worthy performance. I can see how my father was so taken in by you."

"Were I you, Mr. Sage," Bennett Tarrant interjected, "I would be careful what I said to the woman who owns the Long Island mansion my mother calls home."

It hit Gracie then, finally, just how much power she wielded at the moment. Legally, she could indeed toss Vivian Sage into the street and move into the Long Island house herself. That was what a trashy, scheming, manipulative gold digger who'd used her sexual wiles to take advantage of a fragile old man would do.

So she said, "Mr. Tarrant, what do I have to do to deed the Long Island house and everything in it to Mrs. Sage? This is her home. She should own it, not me."

Harrison Sage eyed Gracie warily at the comment, but he said nothing. Something in Vivian's expression, though, softened a bit.

"It's just a matter of drawing up the paperwork," Mr. Tarrant said. "Today being Wednesday, we could have everything ready by the end of next week. If you don't mind staying in the city for a little while longer."

Gracie expelled a soft sigh. Harry's Long Island estate had to be worth tens of millions of dollars, and its contents worth even more. Just shedding that small portion of his wealth made her feel better.

"I don't mind staying in the city awhile longer," Gracie said. "It'll be fun. I've never been to New York before. Could you recommend a hotel? One that's not too expensive? The one I'm in now is pretty steep, but I hadn't planned to stay more than a couple of nights."

"It's New York City, Gracie," Mr. Tarrant said with a smile. "There's no such thing as *not too expensive*."

"Oh, you don't want to stay in the city," Vivian said. "Darling, it's so crowded and noisy. Spend the time with us here in the Hamptons. It's beautiful in June. We've been having *such* lovely evenings."

Harrison looked at his mother as if she'd grown a second head. "You can't be serious."

Gracie, too, thought Vivian must be joking. A minute ago, she'd looked as if she wanted Gracie to spontaneously combust. Now she was inviting her to stay at the house? Why? So she could suffocate Gracie in her sleep?

"Of course I'm serious," Vivian said. "If Grace— you don't mind if I call you Grace, do you, darling?— is kind enough to give me the house, the least I can do is make her comfortable here instead of having her stay in a stuffy old hotel in the city. Don't you think so, Harrison?"

What Harrison was thinking, Gracie probably didn't want to know. Not if the look on his face was any indication.

"Please, Grace?" Vivian urged. "We've all gotten off on the wrong foot. This just came as such a shock, that's all. Let us make amends for behaving badly. You can tell us all about how you met my husband and what he was like in Cincinnati, and we can tell you about his life here before you met him."

Gracie wasn't sure how to respond. Was Vivian really being as nice as she seemed? Did she really want to mend fences? Or was there still some potential for the suffocation thing?

Gracie gave herself a good mental shake. She'd been a billionaire for barely a week, and already she was seeing the worst in people. This was exactly why she didn't want to be rich—she didn't want to be suspicious of everyone she met.

Of course Vivian was being nice. Of course she wanted to make amends. And it *would* be nice to hear about Harry's life before Gracie met him. She'd always thought the reason he didn't talk about himself was because he thought she'd be bored. His life must have been fascinating.

For some reason, that made Gracie look at Harrison

again. He was no longer glowering at her, and in that moment, she could see some resemblance between him and his father. They had the same blue eyes and square jaw, but Harrison was a good three inches taller and considerably broader in the shoulders than Harry had been. She wondered if he had other things in common with his father. Did he share Harry's love of baseball or his irreverent sense of humor? Did he prefer pie to cake, the way his father had? Could he cook chili and fox-trot with the best of them?

And why did she suddenly kind of want to find out?

"All right," she said before realizing she'd made the decision. "It's nice of you to open your home to me, Mrs. Sage. Thank you."

"Call me Vivian, darling," the older woman replied with a smile. "I'm sure we're all going to be very good friends before the week is through."

Gracie wasn't so sure about that. But Vivian seemed sincere. She, at least, might turn out to be a friend. But Harrison? Well. With Harrison, Gracie would just hope for the best.

And, of course, prepare for the worst.

Three

Gracie awoke her second day on Long Island feeling only marginally less uncomfortable than she had on her first. Dinner with Vivian last night—Harrison was, not surprisingly, absent—had been reasonably polite, if not particularly chatty on Gracie's part. But she still felt out of place this morning. Probably because she was out of place. The bedroom in which Vivian had settled her was practically the size of her entire apartment back in Seattle. Jeez, the bed was practically the size of her apartment back in Seattle. The ceiling was pale blue with wisps of white clouds painted on one side that gradually faded into a star-spattered twilight sky on the other. The satiny hardwood floor was scattered with fringed flowered rugs, and the furniture and curtains could have come from the Palace at Versailles.

How could Harry have lived in a house like this?

It was nothing like him. His apartment had been furnished with scarred castoffs, and the rugs had been threadbare. His walls had been decorated with Cincinnati Reds memorabilia, some vintage posters advertising jazz in Greenwich Village and a couple of paint-by-number cocker spaniels. And Harry had loved that apartment.

There had been no ocean whispers drifting through the windows in the old neighborhood. No warm, salt-laden breezes. No deserted beaches. No palatial homes. There had been tired, well-loved old houses crowded together. There had been broken sidewalks with violets growing out of the cracks. There had been rooms crammed with remnants of lives worked hard, but well spent, too. Life. That was what had been in her and Harry's old neighborhood. Real life. The sort of life she'd always lived. The sort of life she'd assumed Harry had lived, too.

Why had a man who could have had and done anything he wanted abandoned it all to live in a tiny apartment in a working-class neighborhood six hundred miles away? Harry Sagalowsky, alleged retired TV repairman, had turned out to be quite the mystery man.

For some reason, that thought segued to others about Harry's son. Harrison Sage was kind of a mystery, too. Was he the charming flirt she'd first met in the library yesterday? Or was he the angry young man who was convinced she had taken advantage of his father? And why was it so important that she convince him she wasn't like that at all?

Today would be better, she told herself as she padded to the guest bathroom to shower. Because today she and Harrison—and Vivian, too—would have a chance to get to know each other under better circumstances. They would get to know each other period. It was a new day. A day to start over. Surely, Harrison Sage would feel that way, too. Surely, he would give her a chance to prove she was nothing like the person he thought she was.

Surely, he would.

Harrison was deliberately late for breakfast, hoping that by the time he showed up, Grace Sumner would have left, miffed to be shown so little regard now that she was richer and more important than 99 percent of the world. Instead, when he ambled out to the patio, freshly showered and wearing a navy blue polo and khakis more suitable for playing golf than for being intimidating, he found her sitting poolside with his mother. Even worse, the two women were laughing the way women did when they realized they had some shared experience that had gone awry.

And damned if Grace Sumner didn't have a really nice laugh, genuine and uninhibited, as if she laughed a lot.

His mother sat on one side of the table, still in her pajamas and robe. Grace sat on the other, looking nothing like a gold digger and very much like a girl next door. At least, she looked like what Harrison figured a girl next door was supposed to look like. It was the way girls next door always looked in movies, all fresh and sweet and innocent. He'd never seen an actual girl next door who looked like that, since the girls he'd grown up with who lived next door—a half mile down the beach—had always looked…well, kind of like gold diggers, truth be told.

But not Grace Sumner. Her burnished hair was
in a ponytail today, the breeze buffeting a few loose
strands around her nape and temple in a way that made
Harrison itch to tuck them back into place, just so he
could watch the wind dance with them again. Her flawless face was bathed in late morning sunlight, making her skin rosy. The retro suit of the day before had
been replaced by retro casual clothes today—a sleeveless white button-up shirt and those pants things that
weren't actually pants, but weren't shorts, either, and
came to about midcalf. Hers were spattered with big,
round flowers in yellow and pink. Her only jewelry was
a pink plastic bracelet that had probably set her back at
least two dollars. Maybe as much as three.

Had he not known better, he could almost believe she was as innocent of conning his father as she
claimed. He would have to stay on guard around her.
Would that his father had been as cautious, none of this
would be happening.

"Oh, Harrison, there you are!" his mother called
out when she saw him. "Come join us. We saved you
some caviar—mostly because Gracie doesn't like caviar. Can you imagine?"

No, Harrison couldn't imagine a woman who had
just swindled herself billions of dollars not liking caviar. But it was an acquired taste for some people. She'd
get the hang of it once she was firmly entrenched in the
new life she'd buy with his family's money.

"And there's still some champagne, too," his mother
continued. "Gracie doesn't like mimosas, either."

Neither did Harrison. Still, he would have expected
someone like Grace to lap up champagne in any form
from her stiletto. The thought made his gaze fall to

her feet. She wore plain flat shoes—pink, to match the flowers on her pants.

Okay, that did it. No woman could be as adorable and unsullied as Grace Sumner portrayed herself. It just wasn't possible in a world as corrupt and tainted as this one. He stowed what little sentimentality he had—which, thankfully, wasn't much—and armed himself with the cynicism that was so much more comfortable.

Yeah. That felt better.

"Good morning," he said as he took his seat between the women.

"It *is* a good morning," his mother replied. "I slept so much better last night, thanks to Gracie."

Gracie, Harrison repeated to himself. His mother had tossed out the diminutive three times now. It was the sort of nickname any self-respecting girl next door would invite her new best friends to use. Great. His mother had fallen under her spell, too.

"You missed a wonderful dinner last night," she added. "Gracie is giving us the Park Avenue penthouse and everything in it, too. She's already called Mr. Tarrant about it. Isn't that nice of her?"

Harrison's gaze flew to Grace, who was gazing back at him uncomfortably.

"Really," he said flatly.

His tone must have illustrated his skepticism, because Grace dropped her gaze to the fingers she'd tangled nervously atop the table. The plate beside them held the remnants of a nearly untouched breakfast. In spite of her having looked like she was enjoying herself with his mother, she was clearly uneasy.

"It's the right thing to do," she said, still avoiding

his gaze. "Harry would have wanted his family to keep the places they call home."

"The right thing to do," Harrison told her, "would be to return everything my father left you to the family who should have inherited it in the first place."

That comment, finally, made Grace look up. "Harry wanted me to give his money to worthy causes," she said. "And that's what I'm going to do."

"When?" Harrison asked.

"As soon as I get back to Seattle. I want to meet with a financial consultant first. I have no idea what to do at this point."

Of course she wanted to meet with a financial consultant. She needed to find out how to bury that much money so deep in numbered and offshore accounts that no one would be able to find it after the new appeal ruled in the Sages' favor. Which reminded him...

Harrison turned to his mother. "I spoke with our attorney this morning. He's hired the private detective we talked about, to explore this new...avenue."

Vivian said nothing, only lifted the coffeepot to pour Harrison a cup. Grace, however, did reply.

"You're wasting your money," she said. "Not only is this...new avenue...pointless, but I'll be happy to tell you anything you want to know about me."

He studied her again—the dark, candid eyes, the bloom of color on her cheeks, the softly parted lips. She looked the same way she had yesterday when she first caught his eye, the moment she walked into the library. He couldn't remember ever reacting to a woman with the immediacy and intensity he had when he'd met her. He had no idea why. There had just been...something…about her. Something that set her apart from everyone else in the room.

At the time, he'd told himself it was because she wasn't like anyone else in the room. His joke about the pack of bloodthirsty jackals hadn't really been much of a joke. That room had been filled with predators yesterday, which anyone who'd spent time with Park Avenue lawyers and socialites could attest to. And Grace Sumner had walked right into them like a dreamy-eyed gazelle who hadn't a clue how rapacious they could be. It was that trusting aspect that had gotten to him, he realized now. Something in that first moment he saw her had made him feel as if he could trust her, too.

And trust was something Harrison hadn't felt for a very long time. Maybe he never had. Yet there she had been, making him feel that way without ever saying a word. Now that he knew who she really was…

Well, that was where things got even weirder. Because even knowing who Grace Sumner really was, he still found himself wishing he could trust her.

He quickly reviewed what he'd discovered about her on his own by typing her name into a search engine. Although she had accounts at the usual social networking sites, she kept her settings on private. He'd been able to glean a few facts, though. That she lived in Seattle and had for a year and a half. That before that, she'd lived in Cincinnati, where she grew up. He knew she'd been working as a waitress for some time, that she was attending college with an early childhood education major—always good to have a fallback in case conning old men didn't work out—and that she never commented publicly or posted duck-face selfies.

It bothered him that her behavior, both online and

now in person, didn't jibe with any of his preconceived ideas about her. An opportunistic gold digger would be a braying attention-grabber, too, wouldn't she? Then he reminded himself she was a con artist. Right? Of course she was. Naturally, she would keep her true self under wraps. That way, she could turn herself into whatever she needed to be for any given mark. Like, say, a dreamy-eyed gazelle who made a mistrustful person feel as if he could trust her.

"All right then," he said, deciding to take her up on her offer. "Have you ever been married?"

"No," she said. But she didn't elaborate.

So he did. "Have you ever been engaged?"

"No," she replied. Again without elaboration.

"Do you have a boyfriend?"

"There's no one special in my life," she told him. Then, after a small, but telling, hesitation, she added, "There never has been."

Her reply was ripe for another question, this one way more invasive than she could have considered when telling him he could ask her anything. And had it not been for his mother's presence at the table, he might very well have asked it: *Does that mean you're a virgin?* It would have been perfect. If she replied no immediately after saying there had never been anyone special in her life, she would have sounded like a tramp. Had she answered yes, at her age, she would have sounded like a liar. Win-win as far as a court appeal was concerned.

Funny, though, how suddenly he wasn't asking because he wanted to use her status against her. He wanted to know about her status for entirely personal reasons. *Was* Grace Sumner a liar and a con artist? Or was she really as sweet and innocent as she seemed? And why was he kind of hoping it was the latter? Not only would it give him the upper hand if he *could* prove she was conning them all, but it would make her the kind of person he knew how to deal with. He knew nothing of sweetness and innocence. No one in his social or professional circles claimed either trait.

"Do you have any brothers or sisters?" he asked, trying a new tack.

She shook her head. "I'm an only child."

"Mother's maiden name?"

"Sumner."

The same as Grace's. Meaning… "No father?" he asked.

At this, she smiled. "Um, yeah, I had a father. Everyone does. Were you absent from health class that day?"

He refused to be charmed by her irreverence—or her smile. Instead, he asked, "What was your father's name?"

Her answer was matter-of-fact. "I don't know."

"You don't know who your father was?"

She shook her head, something that freed another tantalizing strand of gold from her ponytail. "My mother never told me. On my birth certificate, he's listed as unknown."

Okay, this was getting interesting. It wouldn't be surprising to anyone—like, say, a probate appeals judge—to discover that a young woman whose father had been absent when she was a child would, as an adult, turn to conning old men. Even if she hadn't set out to become a professional grifter when she was a little girl, should an opportunity for such present itself when she was older, it wasn't a stretch to see how a woman like that would take advantage of it.

Maybe she was right. Maybe he wouldn't need a private investigator after all.

"What about your grandparents?" he asked.

"I barely remember my grandmother," she said. "She died before I started school."

"And your grandfather?"

"He died when my mother was in high school. My grandmother never remarried."

Oh, this was getting too easy. A pattern had developed of male role models being completely absent from the life of little Gracie Sumner. It didn't take Freud to figure this one out.

Unable to help himself, he spoke his thoughts out loud. "So. Major daddy issues. Am I right?"

"Harrison!" his mother exclaimed.

Whether her reaction was due to anger at his invasive question or worry that it would make Grace change her mind about giving her back her homes, he couldn't have said. Still, he supposed maybe, possibly, perhaps, he had overstepped there.

"Sorry," he apologized. Almost genuinely, too. "That was out of line."

"Yeah, it was," Grace agreed.

Surprisingly, though, she didn't seem to take offense. Certainly not as much as Harrison would have, had he been asked the same question.

"No, Mr. Sage, I do not have daddy issues," she continued evenly. "I come from a long line of smart, independent women who didn't need the help of anyone—least of all a man—to get by."

He was surprised by the splinter of admiration that tried to wedge itself under his skin at her cool reply.

Until she added, "But you should probably talk to someone about your own issues."

He grinned at that. "What issues?"

"The one you have about strong, independent women."

"I don't have issues with women," he told her. "I have issues with *a* woman. A woman who took advantage of my father."

He could tell by her expression that there was more she wanted to say on that matter. Instead, she said, "If you'll both excuse me, I thought I'd take the train into New York today to do some sightseeing, since I may never have the chance again."

Harrison bit back a comment about the private jet and the yacht she owned, thanks to his father, and how she could go anywhere in the world she wanted, whenever she felt like it. Instead, he sipped his coffee in silence and tried not to notice the wisp of dark gold hair that was curling against her nape in a way that made him unwillingly envious. If she were any other woman, he would have reached over and coiled that strand of silk around his finger, then used it to gently pull her face toward his so he could—

So he could nothing, he told himself. Grace Sumner was the last woman he wanted to touch with affection. Or anything else. Even a ten-foot pole.

"That's a lovely idea," his mother said. "You should do some shopping, too. A young girl like you—" She smiled in a way that was kind of astonishing in light of the fact that she'd just encouraged a stranger to go out and spend money that should belong to her. "A young *rich* girl like you," she amended, "should have a closet full of beautiful things to wear. Beautiful *new* things."

The emphasis on the word *new* obviously didn't escape Grace's notice. She glanced down at her outfit, one that looked like something from a sixties flick titled *Beach Blanket Barbie*. Strangely, she didn't seem to think there was anything wrong with it. For a moment, she looked as if she wanted to explain her wardrobe choices, and then seemed to change her mind. Good call, Harrison thought. His mother never kept clothes past the season and year for which they'd been designed.

"Timmerman can drive you to the train," Vivian told her. "Just remember to be back by eight, because Eleanor is making something special for dinner tonight. In your honor."

Somehow, Harrison kept from rolling his eyes. His mother was becoming such a suck-up.

After Grace left, he finished his coffee, downed what was left of the bacon and toast and listened for the car to pull away from the house. Then he headed for his Maserati and made his way to the train station, too.

So Grace wanted to see the sights of New York City. Right. All along Fifth Avenue, he'd bet. Starting with Saks and ending with Tiffany, allowing just enough time for a late lunch at Le Bernardin. Luckily, he'd given himself the rest of the week off—he could do that, being the owner of his own company—to deal with The Sumner Problem, so he had no obligations today.

None except exposing a con artist who was so good at what she did, she could make a man long for things he knew he would never have.

* * *

It was some hours later that Harrison discovered how right he'd been in his suspicions—Grace Sumner did go shopping and treat herself to a late lunch. But only after seeing sights like the Empire State Building, Rockefeller Center and Times Square. And even though that last left her within walking distance of Fifth Avenue, she took the subway to go hopscotching all over Brooklyn. Specifically, through the thrift stores of Brooklyn. And instead of Le Bernardin, she bought her lunch from a Salvadoran food truck.

Grace Sumner was either a con artist of even greater sophistication than he'd thought, or she knew he was following her. And since he was confident he hadn't revealed himself, he was going for the former. Unless, of course, her intentions toward his father's money were exactly what she claimed, and she would be giving it all away, meaning she was on a major budget that prohibited things like Fifth Avenue shopping sprees.

Yeah, right. And maybe tonight, while he was sleeping, the Blue Fairy would fly into his room and turn him into a real boy.

What the hell kind of game was she playing? And how long was she going to play it? Even if—no, when—his detective discovered the truth about her, and an appeals court finally found in the Sages' favor, for now, his father's money legally belonged to her. It could be weeks, even months, before Harrison had the evidence he needed to win the return of his father's fortune. It would take even longer for another appeal in court. In the meantime, she was within her rights to spend every dime.

So why wasn't she doing that? And why was she

staying with his mother on Long Island, away from Bennett Tarrant and his colleagues, who were the only support she had? There was more going on here than a simple con. There had to be. Harrison just needed to figure out what it was. And he would have to do it within a week, since Grace would be leaving after the paperwork was complete to return the estate and the penthouse to his mother. Just who was Grace Sumner—wicked woman or good girl?

And the toughest question to answer of all—why was Harrison kind of hoping it was the latter?

Four

Until she saw it in action, Gracie never would have guessed how closely the New York Stock Exchange after the ringing of the bell resembled the kitchen of Café Destiné after the eighty-sixing of the béchamel sauce. Absolute mayhem. And she wasn't even *on* the floor. She was with Harrison in the gallery above it, looking down as millions of dollars' worth of commodities, futures and options—and, for all she knew, lunches, Pokémon cards and Neopets—were traded, bought and sold in a way she would never, ever understand. Not that Harrison hadn't tried to explain it to her. He'd used every minute of their drive from Long Island doing just that—probably because it kept him from having to talk to her about anything else.

It had been Vivian's idea that he should bring Gracie into the city again today, but for a different kind of sightseeing. Last night, over dinner, when Gracie and Harrison had been gazing suspiciously at each other across the table and responding to Vivian's attempts at repartee with little more than awkward mumbling, his mother had suggested the two of them should spend more time together so that each could get to know the other's version of the man they shared in common.

Gracie figured it was more likely, though, that Vivian was worried about the antagonism that could potentially mushroom between Gracie and Harrison, and how Vivian would then be left homeless.

So Gracie and Harrison had risen extra early to make it to Wall Street in time to hear the Friday opening bell. Early enough that Gracie only had time to consume a single cup of coffee. That had given her just enough presence of mind to at least pretend she understood all the stuff Harrison said about SEC, PLC and OTC—and the stuff about yearlings and bulls and bears, oh my—but it hadn't constituted much in the way of breakfast. Now her UGI was growling like a bear, her mood was fast depreciating and her brain was beginning to liquidate.

Hmm. Maybe she'd understood more of what he'd said than she thought. Despite the downturn of her current market…ah, she meant, body…she tried to focus on what he was saying now.

"My father had a real gift for trading," he told her.

Harrison fit in this world nicely with his dark slate suit and dove-gray dress shirt, but his necktie, with its multicolored dots, was a tad less conservative than the staid diagonal stripes and discreet tiny diamonds on the ties worn by the other men. Although Gracie had tried to dress for business, too, the best she'd been able to do was another vintage suit—the second of the only two she owned. This one was a dark ruby with pencil skirt and cinch-waisted jacket with a slight peplum. She'd thought she looked pretty great when she got dressed. Seeing the other women in their dark grays and blacks and neutrals, she now felt like a giant lollipop.

"His initial fortune," Harrison continued, "the one he used to buy and build his companies, was all earned in the stock market. He never went to college. Did you know that?"

There was something akin to pride in his voice when he spoke of Harry's lack of formal education. It surprised Gracie. She would have thought Harrison was the kind of man who wouldn't want anyone to know about his father's lack of education because it would be an embarrassment to the family name.

"I did know that, actually," she said. "But he told me it was because he couldn't afford to pay for college."

"He couldn't. Not after he graduated from high school, anyway."

"Harry never graduated from high school."

The moment the words were out of her mouth, Gracie regretted them. Not because she worried they would be an embarrassment to the Sage name, too, but because Harrison's expression made clear he hadn't known that. And now he was finding it out from someone he'd just met who had obviously known it for some time.

Nevertheless, he said, "Of course my father graduated from high school. Findlay High School in Cincinnati. Class of fifty-three."

"Harry never even made it to his junior year," Gracie told him. "He dropped out when he was fifteen to work in the Formica factory. He lied about his age to get the job and join the union."

Harrison gazed at her blankly. "Why would he do that?"

Oh, boy. There was obviously *a lot* he didn't know about his father's early life. And Gracie didn't want to be the one to let the cat out of the bag, which, in Harry's case, would be more like freeing a Siberian tiger from the Moscow Zoo.

Gently, she said, "Because by then, Harry's father was drinking so much, he couldn't hold down a job, and his mother was caring for his little brother, so she couldn't work, either. Harry had to be the one to support the family."

At the word *brother*, Harrison's eyes went wide, and Gracie's heart dropped to her stomach. Surely, he'd at least known his father had a brother.

"My father had a *brother*?"

Okay, maybe not. "Yeah. You didn't know?"

Although Harrison's gaze was fixed on hers, she could tell by the emptiness in those blue, blue eyes that his thoughts were a billion miles away. Or, at least, a few decades away. Or maybe he was just trying to decide whether or not to even believe her. But Gracie had seen photos of Harry's family. The old pictures were with his things in the storage unit.

Harrison shook his head lightly, honing his icy blue gaze—which somehow, suddenly, seemed a little less icy—on Gracie again. "But I always thought… I mean he told me… Well, okay he never really *told* me, but I always assumed…" When he realized he wasn't making sense, he inhaled a breath and released it. "I always thought he was an only child. By the time I was born, his parents were both dead, and he never mentioned any other family. Hell, he barely mentioned his parents."

Gracie tried to tread lightly as she told him, "Benjy—that was his little brother—had polio. He died when he was thirteen, and Harry was sixteen. It hit him pretty hard. His mother, too. She left home a year or so later, and Harry never saw her again. He took care of his dad for a couple more years, until he died, too, of cirrhosis. Then Harry left Cincinnati and didn't come back until after he retired from his job as a TV repairman.

"Well, that was what he told me, anyway," she quickly amended. "That he made his living in New York as a TV repairman. Obviously, that part wasn't true. But the rest of it was. When I packed up his things after his death, I found photos and some old diaries that belonged to his mother. I'll be sure everything is sent to you and Vivian once I get back to Seattle."

Harrison eyed her thoughtfully. A little too thoughtfully for Gracie's comfort. He was doing that thing again where he seemed to be trying to peer into her soul. And was succeeding. All he said, though, was "What else did my father tell you about his childhood?"

"He said that after his father died, he took what little money he'd saved and went to New York. TV was just starting to become popular, and he got a job in a little appliance shop and taught himself everything he could. After a while, he opened his own repair business in Queens and lived and worked there until he retired."

"He never mentioned getting married?" Harrison asked. "Three times, at that? Never mentioned having kids? Seven of us?"

She shook her head. "Never. I mean, I always wondered. He never said he *didn't* marry or have a family. But I didn't want to pry. He just told me that after he retired, he started missing Cincinnati, so he moved back to his old neighborhood."

Harrison said nothing in response to that, but he continued to look at Gracie in that way that made something hot and gooey eddy in her belly, melting bit by bit until it warmed her all over. How could he make her feel like that? He'd made no secret of the fact that he didn't trust her. He didn't even like her. Except for their initial meeting, the time the two of them had shared together had been combative at worst and uncomfortable at best. There should be no hot gooeyness in a situation like that.

But maybe that was the problem. Not the unpleasant times since the two of them met. But the handful of moments when the two of them had first encountered each other in the library. Something had definitely blossomed between them in those moments, and it had been anything but unpleasant. Those moments had been some of the sweetest Gracie had ever known. She'd never had a reaction to a man like she'd had to Harrison. Why couldn't the two of them hit Rewind and start over? Go back to that first second when her eyes met his, and she felt as if the pieces of her life that had been ripped apart in the days since meeting Mr. Tarrant had suddenly fallen back into place?

When Harrison still didn't respond to anything she'd told him, she asked softly, "You didn't know any of that stuff about his parents or brother, did you?"

He shook his head.

"What did your father tell you about his childhood?"

"Not much. That he grew up in Cincinnati. That his mother was a teacher and his father worked in a factory. That he used money he saved from a paper route to come to New York after high school."

His expression suddenly changed, moving from quietly preoccupied to fiercely keen. "After his arrival in New York, though, I heard all about that. Over and over again."

"Guess it didn't have anything to do with a TV repair shop, huh?"

He chuckled, but there was nothing happy in the sound. "No. It was all about how he found work as a runner for a brokerage in Manhattan and worked his way up, investing what he could where he could whenever he had a spare nickel. How he made his first million when he was twenty-five. How he bought his first business at twenty-seven. How, at thirty, he was worth tens of millions of dollars. At forty, hundreds of millions. Easy as pie. He had things fall into his lap and then was smart enough to exploit them for all they were worth. Hell, he berated me for not earning my keep when I was a kid. He may have gone into his office every day to keep an eye on things, but as far as actual work? He never worked a day in his life as an adult."

Gracie couldn't help the sound of disbelief that escaped her. "Oh, please. I never met anyone who worked harder than Harry Sagalowsky."

Harrison threw her another one of those dubious looks. "You said he was retired when you met him."

"Yeah, but he was active in his church, he volunteered at the veterans hospital, he served meals at a homeless shelter most weekends and he coached Little League."

She could tell Harrison stopped believing her with the first sentence—he even started shaking his head before she finished speaking. "My father never went to church, he was never in the military, he thought poverty was a scam and he hated kids."

"Your father sang in the choir," Gracie countered. "And he felt a debt to people in uniform because he grew up during a time when a lot of them never made it home from war. I'd think by now you'd realize how he feels about poverty, since he wants me to give away all his money to worthy causes. And I never saw him happier than he was when he was with his team. I bet you didn't even realize what a huge Reds fan he was, did you?"

Now Harrison was the one to utter an incredulous sound. "This just proves I can't trust anything you say. Nothing you've said about my father rings true. Nothing."

"And nothing you've said about him rings true for me, either."

She still couldn't understand how the Harry she'd known could have been a big-shot corporate mogul or abandoned a wife and son. There must have been a reason for it. He'd said in his video that his home life had become unhappy, but that should have made him determined to stay and fix whatever was wrong. Harry really was the finest man Gracie had ever met. So how could he have done things that weren't fine at all?

The tentative moment of…whatever it was she and Harrison had begun to share was gone. And really, did it matter how they felt about each other? Two judges had awarded Gracie Harry's fortune, and she was duty-bound to disburse it in a way that would honor his wishes. It didn't matter if Harrison Sage believed her. It didn't matter if he trusted her. It didn't matter if he liked her. And it didn't matter how he felt about his father, either, since it was too late for any attempts to make amends there. Harry's death had ensured that his son would never have a chance to understand the man beneath the high-powered pinstripes who had walked out on his family fifteen years before. There would be no resolution for that relationship. Ever.

Or would there?

Gracie studied Harrison again, remembering the way he'd been in the library, before their formal introductions. He had reminded her of Harry, she recalled. He had smiled like his father. He'd been as charming. As easy to talk to. He had the same blue eyes and, now that she paid more attention, the same straight nose and blunt jaw. Had circumstances been different, had Harry not been a titan of industry, had he spent more time with his family and given more freely of himself to them, things might have turned out differently for father and son. They might have recognized they had a lot in common. They might have even been friends.

"You didn't really know him, either, did you?" Gracie said softly.

Harrison deflated a little at the question. "The man I knew was nothing like you describe."

"Maybe while he was your father, he wasn't," she conceded. "And that's a shame."

Now Harrison stiffened. "Why is that a shame? My father was one of the most successful men of his time. How can there be anything shameful in that?"

"Because he could have been a successful father,

too," Gracie said. "I wish you'd known the man I did. The Harry I knew was a good guy, Harrison."

It was the first time she had called him by his first name, and it surprised her how easily it rolled off her tongue, and how good it felt to say it. Harrison seemed surprised, too. He opened his mouth to say something, then evidently changed his mind and glanced away. When he did, something—some odd trick of the light—shadowed his eyes, turning the anger to melancholy.

She tried again. "You know, there's a lot of your father in you. I recognized it right away, when you and I were talking in the library the other day."

He turned to look at her again, more thoughtfully this time. "That was who you meant when you told me I reminded you of someone."

She nodded.

"But he and I had nothing in common."

"You look like him."

"Not surprising, since we come from the same gene pool."

"You told me a joke, right off the bat. That was just like something Harry would do."

"That was just like something a lot of men would do if they were trying to impress a—" He halted abruptly, then said quickly, "That was just like something a lot of men would do."

"It still reminded me of Harry."

Harrison returned his attention to the trading floor. "He brought me here when I was a kid," he said quietly. "Once. I was six or seven. He wanted to show me how fortunes were made and lost. He said this—" he gestured down at the chaos below "—was what made the whole world work. He told me money was more important than anything, because it could buy anything. Not just material possessions, but *anything*. Adventure. Culture. Intelligence. It could buy friends. Allies. Even governments. Not to mention things like respect and dignity and love."

Gracie wanted to deny that Harry could have ever been that cynical or said anything that cold. Especially to a child. Especially to his own son. The man she'd known had thought money was what caused all the world's problems, not solved them. And he'd known it was a person's actions, not their income, that garnered respect and dignity and love.

"You can't buy love," she said softly.

Harrison looked at her. "No?"

She shook her head.

He glanced back down at the floor. "Maybe not. But you can buy something that feels like it."

"No, you can't," Gracie countered. "Maybe you can lie to yourself until you believe that, but…"

When he looked at her this time, she was the one to glance away.

"But what?" he asked.

She shook her head again. "Nothing."

He studied her so long without speaking that it began to feel as if he were trying to insert a little piece of himself inside her. What was weird was that a piece of him should feel like a pebble in her shoe. Instead, it felt more like more a ray of sunshine on her face.

"You must be hungry," he finally said.

There was a huskiness in his voice when he spoke that made something in her stomach catch fire. She didn't dare look at him for fear that those blue eyes would be burning, too. How did he do that? How did he make any given situation feel almost…sexual? He'd done it in the library that first morning, and again at breakfast yesterday. The man was just strangely potent.

"A little," she said, hoping her stomach didn't decide to punctuate the statement with the kind of growl that normally preceded a lunge to the jugular.

"My mother suggested I take you to my father's club for lunch," he said. "By the time we get there, they should be ready to serve."

"Lunch sounds great," she told him.

Even if lunch actually sounded like another opportunity for the two of them to find something to be at odds about. At least food would quiet the wild animal that seemed to have taken up residence in her belly.

Now if she could just figure out how to quiet the wild thoughts suddenly tumbling through her brain.

Harrison watched Grace from the other side of the table at the Cosmopolitan Club, doing his best to not notice how, in this place, surrounded by all its Art Deco splendor, she looked like some seductive film-noir siren. Her form-hugging suit, the color of forbidden fruit, was buttoned high enough to be acceptable in professional circles, but low enough to make a man—to make Harrison—want to reach across the table and start unbuttoning it. She'd worn her hair down today, parted on one side to swoop over her forehead, something that only added to her Veronica Lake, femme fatale appearance. All she needed to complete it was some raging red lipstick. As usual, though, she didn't seem to be wearing makeup at all. Meaning she was once again that combination of sexpot and girl next door that made him want to—

Okay, so it probably wasn't a good idea to think further about what her appearance made him want to do. Probably, it was better to look at the menu and figure out what he wanted. Besides Grace, he meant.

How could he want someone who had almost certainly taken advantage of his father and pocketed the family fortune? On the other hand, what did ethics and morality have to do with sex? It wasn't as if Harrison hadn't slept with other women who were ethically and morally challenged.

Wait a minute. Hang on. He replayed that last sentence in his brain. It wasn't as if he hadn't slept with *other* women like that? Meaning that somewhere in his subconscious, he was thinking about sleeping with Grace? When did that happen? Then again, why shouldn't he sleep with Grace? He might as well get something out of this arrangement.

"What's good here?" she asked, bringing his attention back to the matter at hand.

"If you like light, go with the brie salad. If you like sandwiches, try the club. It you want something more exotic, the curried shrimp."

"Oh, that does sound good," she said. She scanned the menu until she found a description, then uttered a flat "Oh."

"What?" Harrison asked.

"There aren't any prices listed on this menu."

He still couldn't decide whether or not she was pretending to be something she wasn't. If this was all an act, then she really did deserve an award. If it wasn't, then she was a pod person from outer space. No one could be this naive.

"You don't know what it means when prices aren't listed on a menu?" he asked skeptically.

"Of course I know what that means," she said. "No one's that naive."

"Then what's the problem?"

"I can't afford a place where the prices aren't listed. The money your father left me isn't mine."

"It is until you give it to someone else." And he still wasn't convinced she would do it.

"But—"

"Look, it's my treat," he interrupted. "I'm a member here, too."

"Oh," she said again. Only this time it wasn't a flat *oh*. This time it was a surprised *oh*. As in "Oh, you have your own money?"

"I do have a job, you know," he replied before she could ask.

"I didn't mean—"

"You thought I was just some lazy, entitled player who never worked a day in his life, didn't you?"

"No, I—"

"I actually have my own business," he said, hoping he didn't sound as smug about that as he felt, but figuring by her expression that he probably did. Oh, well. "Sage Assets," he continued. "We're consultants in financial risk management."

She clearly had no idea what he was talking about, a realization that nagged again at his conviction that she was driven only by money. "Which means what?" she asked.

"We advise businesses and investors on how not

to lose their shirts in times of financial crisis. Or any other time, for that matter. I started the company right after I graduated from Columbia, and it took off right away," he added modestly. Well, sort of modestly. Okay, not modestly at all. "That being a time of financial crisis. And my father wasn't the only one in the family with a gift for trading." Then, because he couldn't quite keep himself from saying it, he added, "I made my first million when I was twenty-three. I was worth tens of millions by the time I was twenty-seven."

Beating his father's timetable on those achievements by years. At the rate he was going, he'd be beating that hundreds-of-millions thing, too, by a good five years. Not that his father had ever realized—or would ever realize—any of those things. Not that that was the point. Not that Harrison cared. He didn't.

Grace didn't seem as impressed by his achievements as Harrison was. Then again, she had fourteen billion dollars. He was a lightweight compared to her.

"Well, for what it's worth," she said, "I didn't think you were a lazy, entitled player who never worked a day in your life."

"No?"

She shook her head. "I figured you had a job."

Only when she punctuated the statement with a smile did he realize she was making a joke. He refused to be charmed.

"Then you did think I was an entitled player."

Instead of answering, she glanced back down at her menu and said, "You know, I do like a good club sandwich…"

Their server came and took their orders, returning with their drinks. Grace reached for the sugar caddy and used the tongs to pluck out four cubes for her tea. After stirring, she took a sip, and then tonged in two more. As if Grace Sumner needed any more sweetness.

It didn't help that she kept glancing around the room as if she'd just fallen off the turnip truck. Of course, the place was pretty impressive. The Cosmopolitan had been built in the Roaring Twenties by a group of rich industrialists so they and all their equally wealthy friends would have a sumptuous sanctuary to escape the wretched refuse of New York. The furnishings were as rich, extravagant and bombastic as they'd been, all mahogany and velvet and crystal, and the current owners spared no expense to maintain that aura of a bygone era. He and Grace might as well have been lunching with Calvin Coolidge.

"I don't think I've ever been in a place like this before," she said. She grinned again before adding, "Unless you count the Haunted Mansion at Disney World."

Harrison smiled back, surprised to discover it felt genuine. Not sure why, he played along. "I wouldn't count that. They let in all kinds of riffraff at the Haunted Mansion, and the dress code is way too relaxed."

She gave the room another assessment and sighed. "I can't imagine Harry here. His favorite place for lunch was Golden Corral. And I never saw him in a suit."

"I don't think I ever saw him in anything but a suit," Harrison said. "When I was a kid, he was always already dressed for work when I got up, and he usually didn't get home until after I went to bed."

"What about on weekends?" she asked. "Or vacations? Or just relaxing around the house?"

"My father never relaxed. He worked most weekends. The only vacations I ever took were with my mother."

She shook her head. "Everything you tell me about Harry is just so not Harry. What happened to him, that he was so driven by work and money for so long, and then suddenly turned his back on all of it?"

Harrison wished he could answer that. Hell, he wished he could believe everything Grace had said about his father was true. But none of it sounded like him. Not the part about having a sick little brother, not the part about his dropping out of school and definitely not the part about coaching Little League or serving meals to the homeless. *Was* she a con artist? Or had she been as much a target of his father's caprice as the rest of them?

"If what you said about my father's childhood was true—"

"You don't think I was telling the truth about that, either?" she interjected, sounding—and looking—wounded.

"I don't know what to believe," he said honestly.

He still wasn't convinced she was as altruistic as she claimed. The return of his mother's house and the Manhattan penthouse were only drops in the ocean when it came to the totality of his father's wealth. She would still have billions of dollars after shedding those. And she hadn't committed any of those billions to any causes yet.

"But if what you said is true," he continued, "then it's obvious why he was driven by money. Anyone who grew up poor would naturally want to be rich."

"Why is that natural?" she asked.

He didn't understand the question. "What do you mean?"

"Why do you think the desire to be rich is natural?"

He was still confused. "Don't you think it is?"

"No. I mean, I can see how it might have motivated Harry, but not because it was natural. A lot of people are content with what they have, even if they aren't rich. There is such a thing as enough."

"I don't follow you."

At this, she leaned back in her chair and sighed with unmistakable disappointment. "Yeah, I know."

He was about to ask her what she meant by that, too, when their server returned to deliver their selections, taking a few moments to arrange everything on the table until it was feng shui-ed to his liking. After that, the moment with Grace was gone, and she was gushing about her club sandwich, so Harrison let her comment go. For now.

"So where else does Vivian want you to take me?" she asked.

"To one of my father's businesses and a prep school whose board of directors he sat on. And tonight one of his old colleagues is having a cocktail party. I was going to blow it off, but my mother is going and insists you and I come, too."

A flash of panic crossed her expression. "Cocktail party?"

"Is that a problem?"

"Kind of. I didn't bring anything to wear to a cocktail party."

"Fifth Avenue is right around the corner."

Her panic increased. "But Fifth Avenue is so—"

When she didn't finish, Harrison prompted, "So...?"

She looked left, then right, to make sure the diners on each side of them were engrossed in their own conversations. Then she leaned across the table and lowered her voice. "I can't afford Fifth Avenue."

Harrison leaned forward, too, lowering his voice to mimic hers. "You have fourteen billion dollars."

"I told you. That's not mine," she whispered back.

Seriously, she was going to insist she couldn't afford a dress? He leaned back in his chair, returning to his normal voice. "My father told you to take some of the money for yourself," he reminded her.

She sat back, too. "I refuse to pay Fifth Avenue prices for a dress when I can buy one for almost a hundred percent less in a thrift shop."

Harrison turned his attention to his plate, where a gorgeous swordfish steak was just begging to be enjoyed. "Yeah, well, I'm not traipsing all over Brooklyn again, so you can forget about going back there to shop."

The pause that followed his statement was so pregnant, it could have delivered an elephant. When he looked at Grace again, she had completely forgotten her own lunch and looked ready to stick her butter knife into him instead.

Very softly, she asked, "How did you know I went to Brooklyn yesterday?"

Crap. Busted.

He scrambled for a credible excuse, but figured it would be pointless. "I followed you."

"Why?"

Resigned to be honest, since she seemed like the kind of woman who would sniff out a lie a mile away, he said, "Because I wanted to see if you would go out and start blowing my father's money. On, say, Fifth Avenue."

"Why won't you believe me when I tell you I intend to give away your father's money the way he asked me to?"

"Because it's fourteen billion dollars. No one gives away fourteen billion dollars."

"I'm going to."

Yeah, well, that remained to be seen. Instead of continuing with their current topic, Harrison backpedaled to the one before it. "Don't worry about the dress. I'm sure we can find a store you like nearby. I'll ask the concierge on our way out."

Which would doubtlessly be the highlight of the concierge's month. Someone at the Cosmopolitan asking where the nearest thrift shop was. The club would be talking about that one for weeks.

Five

Gracie couldn't believe she was standing at the front door of an Upper East Side penthouse, about to ring the bell. How could she have insisted earlier that Harrison go ahead of her to the party so she could shop for something to wear? She was never going to be allowed into a place like this without him. She still couldn't believe the doorman for the building had opened the door for her in the first place—even tipping his hat as he did—or that the concierge hadn't tried to stop her when she headed for the elevator, or that the elevator operator had told her it wasn't necessary when she fumbled in her purse for the invitation Harrison had given her to prove she had been invited into this world. He'd just closed the doors and pushed the button that would rocket her straight to the top, as if that were exactly where she belonged.

This was the kind of place that wasn't supposed to allow in people like her. Normal people. Working people. People who hadn't even had the proper attire for this party until a couple of hours ago, and whose attire still probably wasn't all that proper, since she'd bought it at a secondhand shop.

She couldn't remember ever being this nervous. But then throwing herself into a situation where she had no idea how to behave or what to talk about, and didn't have a single advocate to cover her back, could do that to a person. Even if being thrown into situations like that had been Gracie's entire day.

After leaving the Cosmopolitan Club, she and Harrison had gone to the prep school where Harry had, once upon a time, sat on the board of directors. Interestingly, it was also the school Harrison had attended from kindergarten through twelfth grade, for a mere sixty-three thousand dollars a year—though he'd told her tuition was only forty-eight thousand when he started, so a big "whew!" on that. The kids had worn tidy navy blue uniforms, they'd walked silently and with great restraint through the halls, their lunches had consisted of fresh produce, lean meats and whole-grain breads trucked in from Connecticut and their curriculum had focused on science, mathematics and the classics. Art and music were extracurriculars that were discouraged in favor of Future Business Leaders of America and Junior Achievement.

It had been such a stark contrast to Gracie's public school education, where the dress code had been pretty much anything that wasn't indecent, the halls had been noisy and chaotic during class changes, the lunches had overwhelmingly been brown-bagged from home and filled with things factory-sealed in plastic and the curriculum had been as busy and inconsistent—in a good way—as the halls, with art and music as daily requirements.

So not only had Harry told his son that money was the most important thing in the world, but he'd also proved it by spending all his time making money and sending Harrison to a school more intent on turning its students into corporate drones than in guiding them into something constructive and fulfilling. What the hell had he been thinking?

The headquarters of Sage Holdings, Inc., where Harry had once been the man in charge, had been no better: all antiseptic and barren, in spite of being filled with workers. Workers who had spoken not a word to each other, because they'd all been confined to cubicles and hunched over computers, tap-tap-tapping on their keyboards with the diligent dedication of worker bees. How could Harry have made his employees work in such soul-deadening surroundings?

And would this party tonight reinforce her anti-Harry Sagalowsky feelings as much as the rest of today had?

Gracie inhaled a deep breath and released it, telling herself everything was going to be fine. She was fine. Her attire was fine. She'd been enchanted by the dress the moment she saw it, a pale mint confection of silk with a frothy crinoline underskirt, a ruched neckline and off-the-shoulder cap sleeves. She'd found accessories at the shop, too—plain pearly pumps and a clutch and a crystal necklace and earrings, along with a pair of white gloves that climbed midway between wrist and elbow. And she'd managed to twist her hair into a serviceable chignon and applied just enough blush and lipstick to keep herself from being as pale as... well, as pale as a woman who was about to enter a situation where she had no idea how to behave or what to talk about.

With one final, fortifying inhale-exhale—*for God's sake, Gracie, just breathe*—she pushed her index finger against the doorbell. Immediately, the door opened, and she was greeted by a smiling butler. Though his smile didn't look like a real smile. Probably, it was a smile he was being paid to smile.

Wow. Harry was right. Money really could buy anything.

No, it couldn't, she immediately reminded herself. Money hadn't been able to buy Gracie, after all. Not that Devon Braun and his father hadn't tried once upon a time.

Wow. Where had that memory come from? She hadn't given a thought to those two scumbags for a long time. And she wouldn't think about them tonight, either. This party would be nothing like the one that set those unfortunate events in motion.

She opened her purse to retrieve her invitation, since butlers were obviously way too smart to allow someone entry just because she was wearing a vintage Dior knockoff and a serviceable chignon. But even though the purse was roughly the size of a canapé, she couldn't find what she was looking for. Just her lipstick and compact in case she needed to refresh her makeup, her driver's license in case she got hit by a bus, and the paramedics needed to identify her body, and her debit card in case Harrison shoved her out of the car in a sketchy part of town and she needed to take a cab back to Long Island, which could happen, since he still didn't seem to believe her intentions toward Harry's fortune were honorable. But no invitation.

She must have dropped it in the elevator when she was fumbling to get it out of her purse the first time. She was about to turn back that way when the same dark, velvety voice that had rescued her from the crowd at the reading of Harry's will saved her again.

"It's all right, Ballantine," Harrison said from behind the butler. "She's with me."

She's with me. Somehow, Harrison made it sound as if she really was *with him*. In a romantic, intimate sense. A tingle of pleasure hummed through her.

Although Gracie had had boyfriends since she was old enough to want one, none had ever been especially serious. Well, okay, that wasn't entirely true. There had been one a while back who'd started to become serious. Devon Braun. A guy she'd met at a party she attended with a friend from school. A guy who'd taken her to a lot of parties like this one, since his family had been rich. But Devon had been sweeter and less obnoxious than most of the guys who came from that background. At least, Gracie had thought so then. For a couple of months, anyway.

But she wasn't going to think about that—about him—tonight. She'd done extremely well shoving him to the back of her brain since leaving Cincinnati, and she wasn't about to let him mess things up now. Tonight she was with Harrison. He'd just said so. And even if they went back to their wary dancing around each other tomorrow, she intended to avoid any missteps tonight.

Unfortunately, she was barely two steps past Ballantine the butler when she began to wonder if she'd

been premature in her conviction. Because the minute
Harrison got a good look at her, his smile fell. Somehow, Gracie was positive his thoughts just then were
something along the lines of how he couldn't believe
she'd shown up dressed the way she was.

When she looked past him into the room, she realized
why. Although all the men were dressed as he was—in
dark suits and ties—none of the women was dressed like
her. Nearly all of them were wearing black, and although
there were one or two bursts of taupe, there wasn't any
clothing in the entire room that could have been called
colorful. Or frothy. Or a confection. Except for a bub-
bly bit of pale mint silk on a woman who looked and
felt—and was—completely out of place.

She forced her feet forward, manufacturing a smile
for Ballantine as she passed him that was no more
genuine than his, and made her way toward Harrison,
whose gaze never left her as she approached.

Although she was pretty sure she already knew the
answer to the question, she greeted him by asking, "Is
there something wrong?"

He gave her a quick once-over, but didn't look quite
as stunned this time. She decided to take it as a compliment.

"Why do you ask?" he replied.

She lifted one shoulder and let it drop. "You look
like there's something wrong."

Instead of giving her the once-over this time, he
simply studied her face. "You look…"

Here it comes, Gracie thought, bracing herself.

"…different," he said.

It wasn't the word she'd expected. Nor did she understand why he chose it. She hadn't done anything

different today from what she'd done every other day he'd seen her. Maybe she'd put on a little more makeup and expended more effort on her hair, but what difference did that make?

"Good different or bad different?" she asked.

He hesitated, then slowly shook his head. "Just... different."

"Oh. Should I leave?"

At this, he looked genuinely surprised. "No. Of course not. Why would you even ask that?"

"Because you seem to think—"

"Gracie, darling!"

The exclamation from Vivian Sage came just in time, because Harrison looked like he wanted to say something else that was probably better left unsaid. Vivian looked smashing, her black dress a sleeveless, V-necked number that was elegant in its simplicity and sumptuous in its fabric. She carried a crystal-encrusted clutch in one hand and a cocktail in the other. She stopped in front of Gracie, leaning in to give her one of those Hollywood air kisses on her cheek before backing away again.

"Darling, you look absolutely adorable," she said. "You could be me when I was young. I think I had a dress just like that."

Of course she did. Except Vivian's would have had a genuine Dior tag sewn inside it, instead of one that *looked* like it said, Christian Dior Paris, but, upon close inspection, really said, Christina Diaz, Paramus. But Vivian had uttered the compliment sincerely, so maybe the evening wouldn't be so horrible, after all.

Then she had to go and ruin that possibility by turning to her son and saying, "Doesn't she look beautiful, Harrison?"

But he surprised Gracie by saying, "Uh, yeah. Beautiful."

Unfortunately, he dropped his gaze to the floor before saying it, thereby making it possible that he was talking about their host's carpet selection instead. Which, okay, was pretty beautiful, all lush and white, like the rest of the room.

This time, when Vivian leaned in, it was toward Harrison. "Then tell her, darling. A woman wants to be reassured that she's the most beautiful woman in the room, especially when she's at one of Bunny and Peter's parties." To Gracie, she added, "Bunny Dewitt is one of New York's biggest fashion icons. She's always being written up in the style section. Every woman here is worried that she's underdressed or overdressed or wearing something so five-minutes-ago."

Then Gracie had nothing to worry about. Her dress wasn't so five-minutes-ago. It was so five-decades-ago. She felt *so* much better now.

Harrison threw his mother a "thanks a lot, Mom" smile at her admonishment, but said, "You look beautiful, Grace."

He was looking right at her when he spoke, and for once, his expression wasn't inscrutable. In fact, it was totally, uh, scrutable. His blue eyes were fairly glowing with admiration, and his mouth was curled into the sort of half smile that overcame men when they were enjoying something sublime. Like a flawlessly executed Hail Mary pass. Or a perfectly grilled rib eye. Or a genuinely beautiful woman.

Then the *Grace* at the end of the sentiment hit her.

Nobody had ever called her Grace. Except for Devon, who'd told her she was too classy to be called Gracie— then turned out to be the most déclassé person on the planet. But she wasn't going to think about Devon tonight, so he didn't count.

And even if Harrison didn't think she was beautiful—or classy, for that matter—the fact that he was making an effort to…well, whatever he was making an effort to do…was a welcome development.

So she replied, "Thank you. And call me Gracie. No one calls me Grace." Well, except for the aforementioned—

Dammit, why did Devon keep popping into her head tonight? With no small effort, she pushed thoughts of the past to the back of her brain again, where they belonged. *And stay there.*

Harrison looked like he wanted to balk at calling her Gracie, but he dipped his head in acknowledgement that he had at least heard her.

"Ms. Sumner!"

Gracie was surprised—and delighted—to hear another familiar voice, and smiled when she turned to greet Gus Fiver, the second-in-command at Tarrant, Fiver & Twigg. He was dressed as conservatively as all the other suits at the party, but there was something about his blond good looks that made him seem far more relaxed. Instead of the briefcase she'd always seen him armed with before, this time he held a cut-crystal tumbler with what looked to Gracie's trained eye like two fingers of very good single-malt Scotch.

"Mr. Fiver," she greeted him. "What are you doing here?"

"Mr. and Mrs. Dewitt's son Elliot is one of my best

friends," he said. "Our families go way back. And please call me Gus."

Gracie turned to include Harrison and Vivian in the conversation, and then realized she had no idea how to do that. Although everyone in the small group knew each other already, it wasn't like the Sages and Tarrant, Fiver & Twigg were exactly best friends. "You, um, you remember the Sages, I'm sure."

Although there was a bit of a temperature drop not unlike the one she'd experienced in the Sages' library a few days ago, Harrison and Gus managed to exchange civil greetings. Vivian was a bit warmer, but she, too, was reserved. Gracie supposed it was the best any of them could manage, having been on opposite sides of a very contentious case for two years.

"I'm surprised to see you here," Gus said. Somehow, though, Gracie couldn't help thinking that the subtext of his sentence was something along the lines of "I thought by now one of the Sages would have suffocated you in your sleep." "I hope you've been enjoying your stay in the Hamptons."

"I have," she said, surprised to realize it was true. In spite of the weirdness of the situation and the wariness of the sort-of truce that seemed to have developed between her and Harrison—at least for now—her stay had been reasonably pleasant and abundantly enlightening. "Long Island is beautiful, and I'm learning all kinds of things about Harry I never knew before. Vivian and Harrison have been very accommodating."

"Vivian and Harrison." Gus echoed her use of their first names in the kind of speculative tone he might have used if he were conjecturing about the identity of Jack the Ripper. "I see."

Gracie supposed it was only natural that he would be skeptical. After all, the last time she'd seen him, Harrison had been accusing her of giving his father an STD and robbing him blind. Now that she thought about it, she, too, wondered why she wasn't still mad at Harrison.

In a word, hmm.

"I'm glad to hear it," Gus said. "And you'll be glad to know—as will you, Mrs. Sage—that the paperwork on the Long Island house and the Manhattan pent-house is in progress. We should be able to courier the papers to you in Amagansett Thursday or Friday, right on schedule."

"That is wonderful news," Vivian agreed. "Thank you again, Gracie."

"No thanks are necessary, Vivian. I'm sure Harry knew I would return the houses to you and that it's what he wanted."

"Yes, well, that makes one of us, darling. Oh, look, there's Bunny," Vivian said, lifting a hand in greeting to their hostess. "You'll all excuse me."

She hurried off without awaiting a reply, leaving Gracie to be the buffer between her son and the law firm that was her son's biggest antagonist.

"So, Gus," she said, grappling for some benign subject to jump-start the conversation. "How did you get into the long-lost-relative business?"

"Tarrant and Twigg recruited me when I was still at Georgetown law school. I was in my last year of pro-bate law and wrote a paper on how to better employ the internet for heir hunting for one of my classes. My professor was a friend of Bennett's and thought he'd find it interesting so he passed it along to him. The next time Bennett was in DC, he and I met for lunch, and he offered me an associate position."

"So have you guys reunited lots of families?" she asked.

"Or split a lot of them up?" Harrison interjected.

Gracie threw him an irritated look, but Gus only chuckled.

"No, it's a fair question," he said. "Family estates can be very contentious, especially when they're large. Fortunately for us, we most often deal with single heirs to estates. Ones who are the last in a line, so there's no one to contest the terms."

"Well then," Harrison said, "aren't my mother and I lucky to be among the few, the proud, the contested."

Again, Gus smiled. "Well, we do seem to have had an unusual run lately of clients who could be wandering into some potential conflict. Once we find them, of course."

"And I'm sure you'll find them," Gracie said.

"We always do," Gus assured her. Then his expression changed. "Well, except for that once."

Gracie was about to ask him more about that, but someone hailed him from the other side of the room. So Gus bid her and Harrison a hasty farewell and made his way in that direction, leaving the two of them alone. And although they had been alone together pretty much all day with fairly little uneasiness, Gus's departure left Gracie feeling very uneasy indeed.

Harrison seemed to share her discomfort, because the moment his gaze met hers, he quickly glanced off to the right, and then turned his entire body in that direction. In response, Gracie turned away and shot her gaze in the opposite direction. Then both of them looked back at each other again, turning their bodies back a little, then a little more, until they were standing face-to-face again. For one long moment, they just stood that way, their gazes locked, their tongues tied. And then...

Then something really weird happened. It was as if some kind of gauzy curtain descended around them on all sides, separating them from everyone else in the room. Everyone else in the world. The clamor of the chattering people tapered to a purr of something faint and almost melodic. The gleam of the chandelier mellowed to a blush of pink. The chill of the air conditioning ebbed to a caress of awareness. And everything else seemed to recede until it was nothing but shadows and murmurs.

Gracie had no idea if Harrison felt it, too, but he stood as still and silent as she, as if he was just as transfixed and didn't want to move or speak for fear of ruining the moment, either. Time seemed to have stopped, too, as if nothing but that moment mattered. Then a woman somewhere in the room barked raucously with laughter, and the entire impression was gone.

Leaving Gracie—and possibly Harrison—feeling more awkward than ever.

"I'll go get us a drink," he said suddenly, sounding almost panicky. Yep, he felt the awkwardness, too. "What would you like?"

Like? she echoed to herself. How was she supposed to answer that? Her brain was so scrambled at the moment, she barely knew her own name, and he was asking her what she wanted? Well, okay, maybe she had an idea of what she, you know, *wanted* at the moment, but there was no way she was going to tell Harrison she wanted *that*. And how could she want *that* from him in the first place? Not only had she known him a mere matter of days, but she also wasn't even sure she liked him enough for *that*. And she was pretty sure he didn't like her, either, even if he was sharing weird, gauzy-curtain, shadow-and-murmur moments with her.

"Um, whatever you're having is fine," she said. "That will be fine. It's fine."

It was all Gracie could do not to slap a hand over her mouth to keep herself from further babbling. For one terrifying second, she honestly thought she was going to tell him that what she wanted was him. Then for another even more terrifying second she thought he was going to tell her that that was good, because he intended to have her. There was just something about the expression on his face just then that—

Thankfully, after one more panicky look, he bolted toward a bar in the far corner of the room, where a group of people had congregated, leaving Gracie alone to collect her thoughts. Unfortunately, her thoughts had wandered so far off that she was going to need an intergalactic mode of transportation to bring them all back.

By the time Harrison returned with their drinks, she had managed to gather herself together enough that her brain and other body parts were reasonably under control. At least until she went to remove her right glove so she could accept her cocktail, because that was when her fingers suddenly wanted to fumble all over the place. Possibly because he seemed unable to peel his gaze away from hers, and then seemed unable to peel it away from her fumbling fingers. After she finally wrestled off the glove, she made a tight fist to halt the trembling of her hand before accepting her drink. But it still trembled when she took the glass from him, enough that he cupped his hand over hers for a moment after transferring the drink to her, to make sure she didn't drop it.

And damned if that weird gauzy-curtain thing didn't happen again. This time, though, they were making contact when it did. She was able to feel how gently he was touching her, and how warm his hand was over hers, and how she wished more than anything he would never let her go. But he did let her go, finally, and up went the curtain again. Somehow, she was able to mumble her thanks, though whether her gratitude was for the drink, the way he touched her or the fact that the strange episode had come to an end, she couldn't have said.

Harrison's gaze met hers again, and he was smiling the same sort of smile he'd smiled when he'd told the butler she was with him. She lifted her drink for a sip and—

Wait. What? The import of that finally struck her. Harrison had been smiling when he told the butler "she's with me." Therefore something about her arrival at the party had made him happy. And something about telling Ballantine she was *with him* had made him happy, too.

Now he was smiling that same smile again, which must mean that he was viewing her less as an enemy. But that was good, right? It meant he was starting to believe Harry left his fortune to her for philanthropic reasons, not because she took advantage of him. So why did Gracie suddenly feel worried again, and for entirely different reasons?

For a moment, they only sipped their drinks in

silence—bourbon, not Gracie's favorite, but it was okay—and looked around the room. Then Harrison fixed his gaze—that blue, blue, good God, his eyes were blue gaze—on hers.

And very softly, he asked, "Earlier tonight, why did you ask if you should leave?"

It took her a moment to remember what he was talking about. Back when she first arrived at the party, when it was obvious he didn't like what she was wearing. "I thought you wanted me to leave because I was going to embarrass you and Vivian."

He looked surprised. "Why would you think that?"

She was surprised by his surprise. Wasn't it obvious why she would think that?

"Because I'm not…sophisticated," she said. "I'm not…elegant. I'm not…" Now she made an exasperated sound. "I don't know how to act around people like this, in situations like this. I don't *belong* here. Not that it ever mattered before, you know? I never needed to be sophisticated or elegant. I never wanted to be. But tonight…"

She trailed off without finishing, and Harrison looked as if he had no more idea what to say than she did. So Gracie sipped her drink again, finding the smoky flavor a little less disagreeable this time. See? People could learn to like things they didn't like before. They just had to give them a chance.

She looked at Harrison again. Harrison, who was so far out of her league, even intergalactic modes of transportation couldn't connect them. No way would he ever consider her sophisticated or elegant or think she belonged in a place like this. She wished she didn't care about that. She wished it didn't matter. She wished…

The irony of the situation was staggering, really. For the first time in her life, Gracie could—technically—afford anything she wanted. And the one thing she was beginning to think she might want was the only thing she would never be able to have.

Seven

The morning after the Dewitts' party, Harrison lay in bed with barely four hours of sleep under his belt, staring at the ceiling and wondering why he couldn't stop thinking about Gracie, who for some reason now seemed exactly suited to that name. Mostly, he couldn't stop thinking about the moment he'd glanced past Ballantine to see her standing at the front door, looking like something that should have been under glass in a pastry shop.

He still didn't know what the hell had happened to him in that moment. He only knew that his stomach had pitched, his mouth had gone dry, his brain had fizzled and his...well, never mind what some of his other body parts had done.

And there had been nothing about her to warrant such a blatantly sexual reaction, which was all his reaction to her had been, he assured himself. Sexual. Even if it had felt like something different. Something more. It couldn't have been anything *but* sexual. She'd just looked so… She'd just seemed so… And he'd felt so… And he'd really wanted to…

He turned onto his side, toward the open window, and glanced at the chair draped with his discarded clothing of the night before. Ah, dammit. He didn't know what he'd wanted when he saw her standing there. Okay, yes, he did know that. What he didn't know was why. Okay, maybe he knew that, too. It had been a while since he'd acted on a sexual attraction. Probably because it had been a while since he'd felt a sexual attraction. All the women he knew were women he *knew*, and once he got to *know* a woman, he pretty much stopped being sexually attracted to her. There wasn't much point in continuing with something once you knew what it was like, and it stopped being challenging. Or interesting. So although Harrison knew *why* he found Gracie attractive, what he didn't know was why he found *Gracie* attractive.

Why her? He'd seen a million pretty girls in a million party dresses in his life. Hell, he'd helped a million pretty girls *out* of a million party dresses in his life. And Gracie wasn't even the kind of party girl he normally went for—the kind who wore lots of makeup and little clothing. What makeup she'd worn last night had whispered, not screamed, and there'd been nothing revealing about her dress. For God's sake, she'd even worn gloves.

Although, now that he thought about it—not for the first time since the night before—her collarbone had looked pretty damned lickable. As had the nape of her neck. And the line of her jaw. And her earlobes...

Really, all of her had looked pretty damned lickable.

He tossed to his other side, punched his pillow, closed his eyes and commanded his brain to grab another hour of sleep. Instead, his brain etched another vision of Gracie on the insides of his eyelids, this one of her looking dashed and asking him, "Should I leave?" He'd been stunned later when she told him she'd asked the question because she thought she was embarrassing him. Because she wasn't sophisticated or elegant and didn't belong in high society.

And all the while Harrison had been thinking how she was more elegant and sophisticated than any of them.

Just who was Gracie Sumner? *Was* she a con artist? Or was she something else?

Harrison bit back a groan. Why was he doubting her? Why was he doubting himself? She *couldn't* be anything other than what he'd suspected since he'd heard the particulars of his father's will. Okay, maybe she wasn't as predatory as he'd first thought, but his father had had too deep an appreciation for money—too deep an obsession with money—to give it all to a stranger and insist that she give it to even more strangers. Harrison Sage, Jr. had been the most calculating, close-fisted man Harrison III had ever known. Philanthropy was the last thing he'd thought about when he was alive. He wouldn't have felt any differently when thinking about his inevitable death. He would have made sure his fortune stayed with the family, where it would grow more obscene, even after he was gone. So what had happened to him to change that?

His father couldn't have been in his right mind when he put Gracie in charge of his personal estate. He had to have been mentally diminished, and she must have taken advantage of that. Maybe she'd convinced him to give his money to charity, and to put her in charge of the funds. And the moment the spotlight was off of her, she was going to take the money and run.

That had to be it. It was the only explanation that made sense.

He was through being enchanted by Gracie Sumner. *Grace* Sumner, he corrected himself. And he wouldn't be swayed by her again.

Gracie was the first to come downstairs the next morning, a not unexpected development, since Vivian had still been at the party last night when she and Harrison left, and Harrison had opted for a nightcap before he went to bed himself. No breakfast had been set up on the patio yet, so Gracie headed back into the house…mansion…palace…most gigantic residence she'd ever seen…to forage in the kitchen herself. She would at least start the coffee, since, as far as she was concerned, a day without caffeine was like a day without precious, life-giving oxygen. As she entered the hall she was pretty sure would lead to the kitchen, however, she crashed into the most gigantic man's chest she'd ever seen. *Oops.*

"Whoa," Harrison said as he wrapped his hands around her upper arms and moved her back a few steps. "What's the hurry? Are we planning to take advantage of everyone's absence to fill our pockets with anything that's not nailed down?"

Ignoring, for now, that neither her red-and-yellow

plaid pants nor her red short-sleeved blouse had pockets—and even if they did, no way could she stuff a Louis Quatorze buffet into one—Gracie frowned at Harrison. When they'd parted ways last night, they'd been on pretty good terms. In spite of some of the weirdness that had arced between them at the party, they'd eventually fallen into a reasonably comfortable fellowship that had lasted all the way through the ride home.

This morning, though, he seemed to want to return to the antagonism she'd thought had vanished. Or at least diminished to the point where he had stopped thinking of her as a thief. She took a step backward, removing herself from his grasp, and frowned harder. Not as easy to do as it should have been, because he looked even yummier than usual in casual dark-wash jeans and a white oxford shirt, the sleeves rolled to his elbows.

Instead of rising to the bait he was so clearly dangling in front of her, she said, "And good morning to you, too."

He deflated a little at her greeting. But he didn't wish her a good-morning in return. Instead, he told her, "The servants get the weekend off. Everyone's on their own for breakfast."

"Which isn't a problem," she said, "except that I don't know where the kitchen is."

He tilted his head in the direction she'd been headed. "You were on the right track. It's this way."

Gracie may have been on the right track, she thought as she followed him through a warren of rooms, but if he hadn't shown up when he did, they would have had to send a search-and-rescue team after her. It struck her again as she absorbed her grand surroundings just how rich Harry had been, just how much he'd turned his back on when he ran away to Cincinnati and just how out-of-place the man she'd known would have been in these surroundings.

Even the kitchen reeked of excess, massive as it was with state-of-the-art appliances—some of them things Gracie didn't recognize even with her restaurant experience.

"Coffee," she said, hoping the word sounded more like a desire than a demand, thinking it came off more as a decree. "Um, I mean, if you'll tell me where it is, I'll make it."

"I set it up last night. Just push the button."

She looked around for a Mr. Coffee, and then reminded herself she was in the home of a billionaire, so switched gears for a Bonavita or Bunn. But she didn't see one of those, either. When Harrison noted her confusion, he pointed behind her. She turned, but all she saw was something that looked like a giant chrome insect. She looked at him again, her expression puzzled.

"The Kees van der Westen?" he said helpfully.

Well, *he* probably thought it was helpful. To Gracie, a Kees van der Westen sounded like something that should be hanging in the Metropolitan Museum of Art. When she continued to gaze at him in stumped silence, he moved past her to the big metal bug, placed a coffee cup beneath one of its limbs, and pushed a button. Immediately, the machine began to hum, and a beautiful stream of fragrant mahogany brew began to stream into the cup.

"Wow," she said. "That's more impressive than the espresso machine we have at Café Destiné." Then, because she hadn't had her coffee yet so couldn't be held responsible for her indiscretion, she asked, "How much did that set you back?"

Harrison didn't seem to think the question odd, however. He just shrugged and said. "I don't know. Six or seven thousand, I think."

She couldn't help how her mouth dropped open at that. "Seven thousand dollars? For a coffeemaker?"

"Well, it does espresso and cappuccino, too," he said. "Besides, you get what you pay for."

"You know what else you can get for seven thousand dollars?" she asked, telling herself it was still because she hadn't had her coffee, but knowing more that it was because she wanted to prove a point.

He thought for a minute. "Not a lot, really."

"There are some cities where seven thousand dollars will pay for two years of community college," she said. "What you think of as a coffeemaker is a higher education for some people."

His expression went inscrutable again. "Imagine that."

"I don't have to imagine it," she said. "I've done a lot of research. Do you have any idea how many lives your father's fourteen billion dollars will change? Any concept at all? Do you even know what *one* billion dollars could buy?"

Instead of waiting for him to answer, she continued, "One billion dollars can send more than twenty-five thousand kids to a public university for four years. Twenty-five thousand! A billion dollars can put two million laptops in public schools. A billion dollars can buy decent housing for six thousand families in some places. A billion dollars can run seven thousand shelters for battered women for a year. You add up how many lives would be improved. And that's only the first four billion."

Harrison's expression remained fixed, but something flickered in his eyes that made her think she was getting through to him.

So she added, "Your father's money can bring libraries to communities that don't have one. It can put musical instruments in schools that can't afford them. It can build playgrounds in neighborhoods that are covered with asphalt. It can send kids to camp. It can build health clinics. It can fill food banks. Maybe that was why Harry changed his mind late in life about what he wanted to do with his money. So he'd be remembered for changing the world, one human life at a time."

At this, Harrison's expression finally changed. Though not exactly for the better. "And what about his family?" he asked. "Did my father have to completely shut us out? You keep talking about him as if he were this paragon of altruism in Cincinnati, conveniently forgetting about how he turned his back on his family here. Not just me and my mother, but my half sisters and their mothers, too. My father spent his life here taking whatever he wanted whenever he wanted it, often from people he claimed to love. Now he wants to give it all back to strangers? Where's the logic in that? Where's the commitment? Where's the obligation? Where's the… Dammit, where's the love?"

His eruption stunned Gracie into silence. Not because of the eruption itself, but because she realized he was right. She'd been thinking of Harry's fortune as an all-or-nothing behemoth, something that either went to charity or to the Sages, and neither the twain should meet. But Harry could have left something to his family. Not just to Harrison and Vivian, but to his ex-wives and other children, too. So why hadn't he?

"I'm sorry," Gracie said, knowing the words were inadequate, but having no idea what else to say. She didn't know why Harry had excluded his family from his will. Maybe he'd figured Harrison would be fine on his own and capable of taking care of Vivian. Maybe he'd assumed his divorce settlements with his exes were enough for all of them and his other children to have good lives. And probably, that was true. But he still could have left each of them *some*thing. Something to show them he remembered them, to let them know he had loved them, even if he hadn't done that in life.

Because one thing Gracie did know. As rough-around-the-edges and irascible as Harry could be, he *had* been able to love. She'd seen him express it every day. Maybe not in his words, but in his actions. He'd loved his parents and little brother once upon a time, too. And if he'd been able to love a family as fractured as his had been when he was a boy, then he *must* have loved Harrison and Vivian, too, even if he'd never been any good at showing it. Maybe if Harrison had known him the way Gracie did, he would be able to see that, too.

If only she could take Harrison back in time a few years and introduce him to the version of his father she knew. If only he could see Harry in his flannel bathrobe, shuffling around his apartment in his old-man slippers and Reds cap, watering his plants, his favorite team on TV in the background, his four-alarm chili bubbling on the stove. If only he could see Harry's patience when he taught her to fox-trot or his compassion when he filled trays at the shelter or his gentleness showing some kid how to hold a bat.

And that was when it hit her. There was a way she *could* show Harrison those things. Harry wouldn't be there physically, of course, but he'd be there in spirit. Harrison had shown her his version of his father in New York yesterday. So why couldn't Gracie show him her version of Harry in Cincinnati? They could fly there tomorrow and spend a couple of days. She could take Harrison to the storage unit to go through his father's things. They could watch the Little League team Harry coached. She could show Harrison the hospital and shelter where Harry volunteered and introduce him to some of the people who knew him. She could even take him dancing at the Moondrop Ballroom.

Harrison had never known that side of his father. Maybe if they went to Cincinnati, he'd see that Harry wasn't the cold, rapacious man he remembered. And maybe, between the two of them, they could figure Harry out, once and for all.

"Harrison," she said decisively, "we need to go to Cincinnati."

His expression would have been the same if she had just smacked him with a big, wet fish. "Why do we need to go to Cincinnati?"

"So you can meet Harry."

"You've already told me all about him."

"And you don't seem to believe any of it."

He said nothing in response to that. What could he say? He *didn't* believe anything she'd told him about Harry. Not really. He was the kind of person who needed to see stuff with his own eyes to be convinced.

"I have to go back to work next week," he said,

lamely enough that Gracie knew that wasn't the reason he was balking.

"You can give yourself a couple more days off," she said. "You're the boss."

He said nothing again, but that only encouraged her. "Look, you took me on the Harrison Sage, Jr. tour of New York City. So now let me take you on the Harry Sagalowsky tour of Cincinnati."

"And did the Harrison Sage, Jr. tour change your mind about your friend Harry?" he asked.

Gracie hesitated before replying. "Not really," she admitted. But she quickly declared, "But it's given me a lot to think about. It's added a lot to my picture of Harry, and even if the things I learned don't paint him in the greatest light, I'm still glad to have learned them. I want to do the same for your picture of Harrison, Jr.," she added more gently. "So you'll have more to think about, too."

This time, Harrison was the one to hesitate. Finally, he told her, "It won't make any difference in the way I feel. About my father or you."

Something in the way he said it, though, made Gracie think he was at least willing to give it a chance. Where his father was concerned, anyway. Although maybe he meant—

"It doesn't matter how you feel about me," she said before her thoughts could go any further, wishing that were true. Wondering why it wasn't. She really shouldn't care about how Harrison felt about her. Her only goal at the moment was to help him move past his resentment toward his father. But she couldn't quite forget those few moments the night before when things had seemed…different between them. And she couldn't forget the way he'd looked when she told him all the things he hadn't known about his father's past. Like a hurt little kid who was just trying to make sense of things and couldn't.

Let me help you make sense of it, Gracie silently bid him. *Of your father and of me. And let me try to make sense of you, too.* Because somehow, it was beginning to feel just as important for her and Harrison to understand each other as it was for them to understand Harry.

Harrison hesitated again. Long enough this time that Gracie feared he would decline once and for all. Finally, reluctantly, he told her, "Okay. I'll go."

She expelled a breath she hadn't been aware of holding. "Great. How long will it take you to pack?"

Eight

Gracie couldn't have ordered a better day for a base-ball game. June was the kindest of the summer months in the Ohio Valley, the skies blue and perfect and the breezes warm and playful. The park where Harry's Little League team, the Woodhaven Rockets, played had four baseball diamonds and every one of them was filled. She and Harrison had arrived early enough to find a bleacher seat in the shade, up on the very top bench, where they could see all the action. She'd instructed him to wear the team colors, so he'd complied with gray cargo shorts and a pale blue polo that made his blue, blue eyes even bluer. She'd opted for white capris and a powder-blue sleeveless shirt for herself.

They'd arrived in Cincinnati the evening before, late enough that there hadn't been time to do much more than say good-night and turn in. Harrison had wanted to have lunch before the game today, but Gracie told him that until she presented the league with a check from Harry's estate, concessions were where they made most of their money for uniforms and equipment, so the least she and Harrison could do was plunk down a few bucks for a couple of hot dogs and sodas. Not to mention if Dylan Mendelson was still on the team, there might be some of his mom's red velvet cupcakes.

The Rockets were leading in the seventh inning four to zip, their pitcher barreling ball after ball over home plate without a single crack of the bat. If this kept up, it was going to be a no-hitter.

"Way to go, Roxanne!" Gracie shouted to the pitcher at the end of the inning as the teams were switching places. "Keep it up, girlfriend!"

When she sat back down, Harrison said, "That's a *girl* pitching?"

"Damn straight. Don't sound so surprised. Girls are great ballplayers."

"No, it's not that. It's that she must not have been on the team when my father coached it."

"Your father was the first one to recognize what a good arm she has. Making her the Rockets' pitcher was one of the last things he did before he died." She brightened. "Now there's a legacy for you. Thanks to Harry, Roxanne Bailey might be the first woman to play in the Majors."

Judging by his expression, Harrison was doubtful. Or maybe it was his father's actions he was doubting.

"What?" she asked.

He hesitated, as if he were looking for the right words. "My father never…cared much…for women."

He seemed to realize Gracie was about to object, so he held up a hand and hurried on. "Oh, he liked women. A lot. My mother would tell you he liked them too much. But he only hired them for clerical positions and never promoted any to executive. He just didn't think women could do anything more than be pretty and type."

"Wow," Gracie said. "That is so *not* the Harry I knew. He put up with a lot of crap from some of the dads for making Roxanne the pitcher, but he didn't back down. And I never saw him speak to a woman any differently than he spoke to a man."

Harrison looked out at the field, but his expression suggested he was seeing something other than a bunch of kids playing baseball.

"Gracie?" a woman called out from behind the bleachers. "Gracie Sumner, is that you?"

She turned to see Sarah Denham, the mother of the Rockets' catcher, standing below them. She, too, was dressed in the team colors, a Rockets ball cap perched backward on her head, hot dogs in each hand.

"Hi, Sarah!" Gracie greeted her, happy to see a familiar face.

"I thought that was you," Sarah said. With a smile, she added, "It's strange to see you without Harry. What are you doing back in town?"

At the mention of Harry's name, Harrison turned around, too, clearly interested in meeting someone else who knew his father in this world. So Gracie introduced the two of them.

"I am so sorry for your loss," Sarah told him. "Your father was one of the nicest men I ever met. He was so great with these kids."

Harrison was clearly surprised by the statement, in spite of Gracie having already told him the same thing.

Sarah continued with a smile, "And his jokes! He kept these kids in stitches."

"My father told jokes?" Harrison asked, startled.

"Oh, my gosh, yes," Sarah said. "What did one mushroom say to the other mushroom?"

Harrison smiled. "I don't know."

Sarah smiled back. "You're a fun guy. Get it? Fungi?"

Harrison groaned. "That's a terrible joke."

"I know," Sarah agreed with a laugh. "They were all like that. The kids loved them." She turned to Gracie. "So where are you living now?"

Gracie's back went up almost literally at the question. Her own past in Cincinnati was the last thing she wanted to revisit, especially in front of Harrison. "Seattle," she said, hoping Sarah left it at that.

But of course, she didn't. "So far away? I mean, I knew things with Devon got bad—"

At this, Harrison snapped his attention to Gracie.

"—but I didn't know you went all the way across the country," Sarah said.

"That's all in the past," Gracie said. Then she rushed to change the subject. "Hey, did Trudy bring any of her red velvet cupcakes?"

"She did," Sarah said. "But they're going fast."

The perfect excuse to escape. "You want a cupcake?" she asked Harrison as she stood. "My treat. I'll be right back."

Before he could reply, she was trundling down the bleachers toward the concession stand. And just as she tried to do whenever Devon Braun intruded into her life, she didn't look back once.

* * *

Gracie hadn't visited the self-storage unit with Harry's things since snapping on the padlock two years ago, so she braced herself for the discovery that everything might be a little musty. And dusty. And rusty. Fortunately, both she and Harrison were dressed for such a development: he in a pair of khaki cargo shorts and a black, V-neck T-shirt, she in a pair of baggy plaid shorts and an even baggier white T-shirt. Each was armed with a box cutter, and they'd brought additional boxes in which to pack anything Harrison might want to ship back to New York right away.

She had deliberately saved the storage shed for the last day of their trip, because it held what was left of the heart and soul of Harry Sagalowsky. After yesterday's game, they'd visited the shelter and hospital where Harry had volunteered, and where many of the people remembered both him and Gracie. Then she and Harrison had had dinner at her and Harry's favorite hole-in-the-wall barbecue joint, where the owner-chef had come out to regale Harrison with stories about how he and Harry had always argued good-naturedly over whose sauce was best. The chef had finally admitted—but only to the two of them—that there was something about Harry's chili he had never been able to duplicate and he was pretty sure it had something to do with the cumin.

Gracie and Harrison had ended the day by retiring to his hotel room with a rented DVD of *The African Queen*, Harry's favorite movie, something that also surprised Harrison because, even though it was kind of a war movie, it had a romance in it, too, and his father had thought the idea of romance was foolish.

Gracie wondered if Harrison thought that, too. For the most part, he didn't seem any more of a romantic than he claimed his father had been, but there had been times over the last couple of days—and times when they'd been in New York, too—when she'd caught him looking at her in a way that was... Or else he'd said something in a way that was... Or the air around the two of them had just seemed kind of... Well. Gracie wasn't sure if the right word for those occasions was *romantic*. Then again, she wasn't sure it was the wrong word, either. Because something about those occasions, especially over the last couple of days, sure had felt kind of...romantic.

That wasn't likely to change tonight, since the last leg of their tour would be at the Moondrop Ballroom, the epitome of old Hollywood romance, where Gracie would try to teach Harrison to dance the way Harry had once taught her.

If, after all that, Harrison still saw his father as a coldhearted, cold-blooded cold fish who hadn't cared about anything but money, then he was a lost cause, and Gracie didn't know what to do. Of course, she still hadn't accepted the coldhearted, cold-blooded cold fish who'd only cared about money that Harrison kept insisting Harry was, so maybe she was a lost cause, too. At least they could be lost causes together.

She had to wrestle with the storage-unit padlock for a few seconds until it finally gave. Then it took both Harrison and her to haul up the big, garage-type metal door. It groaned like a dying mammoth when they did, and the storage unit belched an odor that was a mix of old books, old socks and old man. Gracie gazed into the

belly of the beast, a cinderblock room about twenty feet
wide by twenty feet deep, wondering where to begin.

"I probably should have tried to find Harry's family as soon as he passed away," she said when she realized how musty, dusty and rusty everything was. "But
I truly didn't think he had anyone."

"Was no one at his funeral?" Harrison asked, the
question touched with something almost melancholy.

Maybe there was part of him that still had the capac-
ity to forgive, and even love, his father—or, at least,
think fondly of him from time to time. Although he
might never fully grieve the loss of a man he hadn't
seen in half a lifetime, and hadn't really ever known,
maybe he was beginning to entertain the possibility
that his father wasn't the villain he'd thought him to be.

In spite of his somber tone, Gracie couldn't help
but smile at the question. "There were lots of people.
His visitation was three days long so that everyone
could have a chance to pay their respects. Even after
that, there were still hundreds of people who attended
the funeral."

"But no one from his family," Harrison said, still
sounding pensive. "Not from any of his families."

"In a way, he had family here," Gracie said, hoping
Harrison wouldn't take it the wrong way. She didn't
want to diminish his and Vivian's ties to Harry. She
just wanted to comfort him, and make him realize his
father hadn't been without loved ones when he died.

But Harrison didn't seem to take offense. "That's
not the same," he said. "Someone from his real family
should have been here."

Gracie extended a hand to touch him, waffled for
a moment and then placed her palm gently against his

shoulder. Harrison looked over at the contact, his gaze falling first on her hand, then on her face, but he didn't move away.

"Your father touched a lot of lives, Harrison," she said softly. "He made a difference for a lot of people when he lived here. And he'll make a difference for a lot more when his fortune is given away."

Harrison inhaled a breath and released it. Then, not even seeming to realize he was doing it, he covered her hand with his. "I just don't understand why he felt like he could only do that for strangers."

Gracie didn't understand that, either. There had to be a reason. But they might never know what it was. She looked into the storage unit again. Maybe they could start looking for an explanation here.

She had taken care to organize Harry's things when she stowed them. Furniture on the left, boxes on the right, clothes and miscellaneous in the middle, with two narrow aisles separating everything to enable access. Nearly half the boxes held books and his record collection, mostly jazz and big band. Many of the rest held his accumulation of Cincinnati Reds memorabilia. It was the boxes in front, though, that Gracie wanted to open first. They were the ones that contained Harry's personal items, including the photographs Harrison needed to see.

She strode to the one closest to the front, pressed her blade to the packing tape seam and slid it along the length of the box with a quick *z-z-zip*. Harrison took a few steps into the unit as Gracie finished opening the box and removed a couple of layers of cedar-scented tissue paper. The first thing she encountered underneath was a beer stein from the last Oktoberfest she and Harry attended. She smiled as she lifted it up for Harrison to see.

"Zee?" she said, affecting her best German accent—which, okay, wasn't all that good. "Your papa luffed hiss *Schwarzbier und leberwurst.* He *vas* a real *Feinschmecker."*

Harrison chuckled at that. He even took a few more steps toward her. But all he said was, "Um, *Feinschmecker?"*

"Ja," Gracie replied. Then, returning to her normal voice, she said, "I wanted to slap him the first time he called me that. German isn't the easiest language to figure out."

"So what's a *Feinschmecker?"*

"A connoisseur of fine foods. Okay, maybe beer and liverwurst don't qualify as such. Suffice to say he enjoyed good *Hausmannskost."*

Harrison nodded. And came a few steps closer. "I never knew my father spoke German."

"Very well, in fact," she said. "He grew up in one of the German neighborhoods here."

Gracie held out the beer stein for Harrison to take. It was stoneware and decorated with a dachshund wearing lederhosen and playing an accordion. Gingerly, he closed the last few feet between them and took it from her.

"Harry was good at the chicken dance, too," she said as she released it.

"No," Harrison said adamantly, finally meeting her gaze. He set the beer stein on top of another still-closed box. "You will never convince me my father did the chicken dance."

Gracie picked through some of the other items in

the box. "If you're ever in Seattle, look me up. I have photographic evidence. Oh, look!" she cried as she picked up something else, cutting Harrison off from commenting on the "if you're ever in Seattle" thing. What was she thinking to say something like that? "I gave Harry this for Christmas!"

She withdrew a plastic electronic device the size of a toothbrush that, when its buttons were pushed, lit up, made funny noises and was generally annoying. She handed it to Harrison.

"What is it?" he asked.

"A sonic screwdriver like the one Doctor Who uses."

"But Doctor Who is science fiction. My father hated science fiction."

"Your father loved science fiction." She gestured toward the boxes in back. "There's a ton of Ray Bradbury, Isaac Asimov and Harlan Ellison books in those. You'll see."

Harrison began pushing the buttons on the sonic screwdriver one by one, the same way Harry had on Christmas morning after unwrapping it. Then he grinned. In exactly the same way his father had.

"Okay, here's what I've been looking for," she said when she uncovered the shoebox with Harry's photographs. She began sorting through them, and then was surprised when Harrison reached in, too, and pulled out a handful to look through himself.

"Here," she said, pausing on one. "This is what I wanted to show you. It's your dad and his brother, Benjy, when they were kids."

She handed the black-and-white photo to Harrison. The edges were frayed, the corners bent, and it was creased down the middle, creating a fine white line between the two boys. They were on the front stoop of the brownstone where the family had rented an apartment. Benjy was sitting on a square box nearly as big as he was. Harry had his arm around his brother, and both were grinning mischievously.

"Your dad is on the left," Gracie said. "He was six in the photo. Benjy was three. The box Benjy's sitting on is where the milkman left the weekly milk deliveries. Harry said the reason they're smiling like that is because they just put the neighbor's cat in the box without telling anyone, and with Benjy sitting on it, the poor thing couldn't get out."

Harrison nodded. "Now *that* sounds more like my father."

"He assured me they let it go right after their neighbor snapped the photo, and he promised it wasn't hurt."

She watched as Harrison studied the photo, but his expression revealed nothing of what he might be thinking or feeling. Finally, he said, "That's my dad, all right." After a moment, he added, "And I guess that's my uncle. Or would have been, had he lived."

Gracie sifted through the photos until she found another one. "And here are your grandparents."

Harrison took it from her, studying it with the same scrutiny he'd given the first photo.

"You look just like your grandfather," she said. "He couldn't have been much older in that picture than you are now."

He considered the photo for another moment. "I can't believe my father never told me about any of this. About where he came from, or his little brother, or what his parents were like." Now he looked at Gracie. "But then, I never asked him about any of it when I had the chance, did I? I never took an interest in where he came from when I was a kid. It never occurred to me that his history was mine, too. I know everything about my mother's family. But they're Park Avenue fixtures. They've been rich since New York was New Amsterdam. My father marrying her was the biggest social coup of his life."

"Maybe that was why he never talked about his past," Gracie said. "Maybe he didn't think it could stand up to Vivian's. Maybe he thought you would be ashamed of an alcoholic grandfather and a grandmother who abandoned her only surviving child."

"The same way he abandoned his family," Harrison said softly.

Gracie sighed. "Yeah. I guess so."

He shook his head. "I wouldn't have been ashamed of any of that. I would have felt bad for him. If I'd known how much he lost when he was a kid... How hard he worked to try to keep his family together... How poor they were all along..."

"What?" she asked when he didn't finish.

"I don't know. Maybe it just would have helped me understand him better or something."

Harrison continued sifting through the photos of his father's family—of his family—lost in thoughts Gracie figured she would probably never be able to understand. Thoughts he would never share with her, anyway, she was sure. Funny, though, how there was a quickly growing part of her that really wished he would.

Sunlight was slanting into the storage unit in a long beam of late-afternoon gold when Harrison finally closed the lid on the box of things he wanted to take back to New York with him. The rest could wait for him to have it moved professionally. There was plenty of room in his mother's attic to store everything. Not that he had any idea why he wanted to store it all. There was nothing of value among his father's things. The furniture was old and scarred. The clothes were old and worn out. The knickknacks were old and kitschy. Even the books and records were run-of-the-mill titles that could be found in a million places. For some reason, though, Harrison didn't want to let go of any of them.

So everything Gracie had said was true. Neither she nor his father had made up any of it. Harrison Sage, Jr. really had had a little brother. He'd really dropped out of school to go to work—one of the things they'd found was his first union card, issued when he would have been fifteen. And he really had lost his parents in terrible ways—they'd also found diaries written by his grandmother describing it all. Harrison had scanned a couple of them, but he wanted to read them all in depth when he got back to New York.

As he gazed upon the boxes and bags that held all his father's worldly possessions—or, at least, all the worldly possessions he had wanted to surround himself with as his life drew to a close—Harrison tried to understand how and why his father had lived his life the way he had. How and why a man who'd had *everything* in New York had preferred to spend his last years in a place where he had had nothing.

Gracie's words echoed through Harrison's head. *There were hundreds of people who attended the funeral.* A lot of them were people Harrison had met yesterday. Kids who loved terrible jokes. A World War

Two veteran whose only visitor most weeks had been Harry Sagalowsky, who brought him a magazine and a cup of coffee, then stayed to talk baseball. A homeless mother he'd helped get a job at a local factory, who was then able to move herself and her kids into their own place and start life anew.

Big damn deal.

There would have been *thousands* of people at his father's funeral if he'd died in New York. And they would have *really* known him. They would have known how much he was worth and recognized his accomplishments in the business and financial worlds. They would have known what companies he'd acquired, which ones he had shed and which ones he had his eye on. They would have known which of his latest ventures had been most profitable. They would have known his favorite drink, his favorite restaurant, the name of his tailor. Hell, they would have known who his current mistresses were and where he was keeping them.

But here? What was the value in delivering a magazine or helping in a job hunt or making kids laugh? What difference did it make if Harry Sagalowsky had shared part of his day with others, supplying simple pleasures and favors to people who needed them? Who cared if one person took time to acknowledge another person's existence in the world and share a little bit of himself in the process? What was so great about making a connection with other people to let them know they were important? Who needed to be remembered as a normal, everyday person who made other normal, everyday people happy when he could be remembered as a titan of commerce who'd made billions of dollars for himself instead?

Thankfully, Harrison's spiel was in his head. Because if he'd said those things out loud, Gracie would have read him the riot act. And he probably wouldn't have blamed her. Okay, maybe he was starting to see why his father had wanted to spend his final years here. Because here, with people who didn't know him as Billionaire Harrison Sage, Jr., he could live a life free of that image and be…well, some guy named Harry who did nice things for other people. Things that maybe didn't change the world, but things that made a difference on a smaller scale. Things that would maybe make up for some of the stuff Billionaire Harrison Sage, Jr. did during his lifetime, like putting money ahead of everything else.

Like turning his back on his family.

Not that Harrison thought what his father had done here in Cincinnati would ever make up for that. But he could see where his father might think it would.

"Did you get everything you want?" Gracie asked.

Her question registered on some level, but Harrison didn't know how to answer it. No, he didn't get everything he wanted. There were still answers to some questions about his father. There was still his father's estate. There was still fifteen years of his life that his father could have been a part of but wasn't. And the other fifteen years when his father was around, but not really part of his life, either. And then there was still the most maddening thing of all that he wanted.

There was still Gracie Sumner.

The trip to Cincinnati had been as eye-opening for him where she was concerned as it had been where his father was concerned. A lot of the kids on the base-ball team had responded to her with genuine affec-tion, even begging her to do an impression of a rival coach they must have seen a dozen times before, but still left them rolling with laughter. She'd stopped for five dozen doughnuts before they'd hit the veterans' hospital, and the staff had received them with thanks in a way that indicated it was something she'd done all the time when she lived here. At the homeless shelter, she'd shared fist bumps with a half-dozen men and asked them how things were going. More to the point, she'd listened to each of them when they replied.

And tonight, she wanted to take Harrison to a place called the Moondrop Ballroom. Somehow, he was cer-tain she would know people there, too. And that they would love her the same way everyone else in this city seemed to.

All of these things made him wonder again about this Devon person whose name had come up more than once today—never in a good way. And every time, Gracie's reply had been the same before she'd changed the subject: *that's all in the past.* But how could it be in the past when everyone kept bringing it up?

"Harrison?" she asked.

Only then did he realize he hadn't answered her question about having everything he wanted from the storage unit. "For now," he said. "I'll get the rest of it as soon as I can."

He turned around in time to see her struggling to lift a box that was too wide for her to carry. When she began to pitch backward with it, Harrison lurched to-ward her, grabbing the box from the side nearest him. For a moment, they grappled to stabilize it, and then, as one, they set it down where she had been aiming. That, however, left the two of them standing literally shoulder-to-shoulder, something that each seemed to notice at once, and something that left them both speechless. They were also unable to make eye contact, since every time their gazes met, they glanced away from each other.

Where before the air in the storage unit had just been uncomfortably warm, it suddenly felt like a sauna. It was a really bad analogy, Harrison decided, since it also brought to mind naked, sweaty bodies wrapped in towels. Towels that could be removed with the simple flick of a wrist, thereby allowing lots of other, infinitely more interesting ways for naked bodies to get sweaty.

"Well, that was close," he said. Not that he was talking about the box they'd just saved, but Gracie didn't have to know that.

"Yeah," she said breathlessly.

A little too breathlessly. Maybe she wasn't talking about the box, either. Maybe she'd been having some sauna ideas, too. As if triggered by such a possibility, a single drop of perspiration materialized from behind her ear, rolled along her jaw, then down the front of her neck, before finally pooling in the delectable divot at the base of her throat. Harrison watched its journey with the same single-minded fascination a cheetah might show toward a wildebeest, wanting to pounce the moment the time was right. Like right now, for instance. But Gracie lifted a hand to swipe the drop away before he had the chance. Dammit.

But when his gaze met hers again, he saw that the reason for her reaction wasn't because she'd felt the perspiration running down her neck. It was because she had noticed his preoccupation with it. Their gazes locked for a minute more, and the temperature ratcheted higher. A single strand of damp blond hair clung to her temple, and it was all he could do not to reach for it and skim it back, and then follow his fingers and brush his lips over her damp skin.

"We, uh, we should get going," she said roughly, the words seeming to echo into his very soul. "We have to…to get cleaned up before going to the Moondrop. And we need to have, um…" She hesitated just a tiny, telling moment before finally concluding, "Dinner. We need to have dinner."

Dinner, he echoed to himself. Yes, they would definitely have that before going to the Moondrop. But maybe later, if the stars were aligned—and if they were both still having sauna thoughts—they could have something else, too.

After all, dancing could really work up a sweat.

Nine

Having known the Moondrop Ballroom was one of the places where she would take Harrison, Gracie had packed the dress and accessories she'd bought for the Dewitts' party and instructed Harrison to bring a suit. So it was a surprise when she answered his knock on her hotel room door to find him on the other side wearing a tuxedo. He even had a white silk scarf draped around his neck. She battled the wave of heat that wound through her at the sight of him, so dashing and Hollywood handsome, and the feeling was not unlike the one she'd experienced in the storage unit that afternoon.

And what the hell had that been about? One minute, she'd been about to drop a box on her toe, and the next, Harrison had been staring at her neck as if he wanted to devour her. His damp T-shirt had been clinging to him like a second skin, delineating every bump of muscle on his torso. His dark hair had been falling rakishly over his forehead, his blue eyes had been hot with wanting, and…and… And, well, suddenly, she'd kind of wanted to devour him, too.

"You look…nice," she finally said.

He smiled. "You look beautiful."

"Thanks," she replied, the heat in her belly nearly swamping her.

"So what time does this thing start?"

When Harry was alive, he and Gracie had been regulars at the Moondrop for Fox-trot Fridays, with an occasional appearance for Samba Saturdays and Waltz Wednesdays. Her favorite nights, however, had been Tango Tuesdays, which, as luck would have it, was tonight.

"There's a beginner's hour at seven," she said, "which is where the instructors give some basic lessons for people who've never been dancing before. The main event is at eight. If you want to go early for the first hour, though, we can," she added, thinking Harrison might not be comfortable jumping in with both feet, especially with the tango, since that was probably the hardest dance to know where to put both feet.

"You know what you're doing, right?" he asked. "I mean you said you and my father did this sort of thing on a regular basis."

"Yeah, but Tango Tuesdays tend to be tricky."

He smiled at her unintended alliteration. "But aren't you trained in tango? A tip-top tango teacher I can trust?"

Gracie smiled back. "Totally top-notch."

His eyes twinkled. "Terrific."

Another moment passed where they did nothing but smile and twinkle at each other. Then Harrison, at least, seemed to recall that they had something to do.

"So...do we have time for dinner?"

"Sure."

She gathered her purse and exited, pulling the door closed behind them. When Harrison proffered his arm with all the elegance of Cary Grant, it somehow felt totally natural to tuck her hand into the crook of his elbow. The warmth in her midsection sparked hotter, simmering parts of her that had no business simmering this early in the evening.

Or ever, she hastened to correct herself. At least where Harrison was concerned. That way lay madness.

Maybe this part of his Harry tour hadn't been such a good idea. If this was the way her body reacted when it was just hand-to-elbow contact, what was going to happen when they got into dance mode? Sure, ballroom dancing in its purest form allowed for space between the bodies, but there were still a lot of parts touching. Not just hands and elbows, but shoulders and backs. Waists. Hips.

Yikes.

Then she remembered this was tango Tuesday. Uh-oh. That meant leg contact. Torso contact. Damn. Why hadn't they been in town for open dance night instead, where she could have insisted they do the bunny hop or something? And now she'd gone and told him she would be his top-notch tango teacher. Tsk, tsk.

Note to self, Gracie, she thought as they waited for the elevator—and her stomach did a little cha cha cha. *It's a treacherous tactic, teaching tango to a tempting, um, guy.*

* * *

Stepping into the Moondrop Ballroom was like stepping back in time. Not just because it had been beautifully preserved in all its postwar elegance since opening in the 1940s, but because the people who came here did their best to dress as if they'd been preserved from that period, too. Most of the regulars were elderly, people who remembered coming here or to ballrooms like it when they were young. That was why Harry had liked the Moondrop so much. But many were Gracie's age or younger, newcomers to ballroom dancing who loved the period and wanted to experience the manners and styles of the time, if for just one evening. Even the orchestra dressed the part. The ceiling was painted the colors of twilight with twinkling white lights that looked like stars. Each wall had a silhouette of the 1940s Cincinnati skyline, topped with more stars. Between the décor and the music—the band never played anything written after 1955—it was easy to forget there was another world beyond the front doors.

"Wow, this place is like something out of a movie," Harrison said when they entered, clearly having fallen under the spell of the ballroom as quickly as Gracie had the first time she was here.

"Isn't it wonderful? It's exactly like I remember."

"How long has it been since you were in town?"

She stiffened at his question, even though it was one she'd fielded in one way or another ever since her arrival. "I left six months after Harry's funeral," she told him. "I haven't been back since."

"But you have so many friends here," he said. "I mean, all those people yesterday obviously knew you pretty well. But it sounded like you haven't stayed in touch with any of them."

"That's because I haven't."

"Why not?"

He didn't seem to be asking out of idle curiosity. But she told herself she was imagining things. She was just hypersensitive because of all the questions she'd fielded about Devon since she'd come back.

All she said was "It's complicated, Harrison."

He looked as if he might let it go, but then said, "Because of Devon."

For some reason, hearing that name spoken in Harrison's voice was far worse than hearing it in anyone else's.

"Yes," she said. "Because of him."

"Do you want to talk about it?"

She shook her head. And she told Harrison what she'd told everyone else, what she told herself whenever Devon invaded her thoughts. "That's all in the past."

Harrison looked like he was going to say more, but the band saved her, striking up the first notes of "La cumparsita."

"Well, aren't you lucky?" she said. "You're going to wet your tango feet with the mother of all tango tunes."

He listened for a moment. "I recognize this song. This is in *Some Like It Hot* when Jack Lemmon is tangoing with Joe E. Brown."

And when Tony Curtis was making out with Marilyn Monroe, she thought, but hopefully neither of them would mention that part. Judging by Harrison's expression, though, he was definitely thinking about it. And also judging by his expression, he knew she was thinking about it, too. Damn.

"Shall we?" he asked, tilting his head toward the dance floor, where a number of people were already in full tango mode.

She smiled in a way she hoped was flirtatious. Not that she was flirting with him or anything. She was just keeping in the spirit of the Moondrop Ballroom, that was all. "If you think you're ready for it."

He smiled back in a way that went way beyond flirtatious and zoomed right into bewitching. "I'm ready for anything."

As if to prove it, he extended his left hand, palm up. The moment she placed her right hand against it, he closed his fingers over hers, drew her close and lifted their hands to chin height—his chin, not hers—so her arm was higher. Then he pressed his other hand to the small of her back and drew her body, very firmly, against his. There was nothing tentative in his hold. His confidence was absolute. Her own body's response was just as fierce. In every single place they touched, little explosions detonated under her skin, rushing heat to every other part of her body.

The moment she was in his arms, he assumed a flawless tango stance, placing his right leg between hers and his left alongside her right. Then he began to guide her forward. Well, for her it was backward, since—obviously—he intended to lead. His first step was with his left foot, all fine and good—except for how Gracie's insides were turning to steaming lava— and his next was with his right, which would have also been fine if Gracie had reacted the way she was supposed to and stepped backward.

But thanks to the little-explosions-of-heat thing, not to mention the steaming-lava thing, she wasn't exactly on her game. So his step forward pressed his thigh into the juncture of her legs, and *wow*, talk about an explosion of heat *and* steaming lava. Her entire torso seemed to catch fire and melt into his. Even though she was pretty good at the tango, she stumbled those first few steps, something that made Harrison splay his fingers wide on her back and pull her closer still, and— *Oh. My. God. She was going to spontaneously combust!* After that, it was all Gracie could do to just try and keep up with him.

He led her deeper into the crowd of other dancers with a few perfectly executed *barridas*, sweeping his feet along the floor in a way that made hers move that way, too. Then he spun them in a perfect *boleo*, punctuating the move with a beautiful *gancho*, wrapping his leg briefly around hers before turning her again. Then he threw in a *lápiz,* tracing a circle on the floor with his free foot—he was just showing off now—and followed with a *parada*, where he suddenly stopped, literally toe-to-toe with her, to perform a really delicious *caricia*. He drew his leg slowly up along hers, then pushed it slowly back down again, generating a luscious friction. She wished he would do it again, and he did. Then he did it again. And again. And—holy mother of mackerel—again.

By now Gracie's heart was hammering hard inside her chest, even though they'd only been dancing a matter of minutes, and he'd been doing most of the work. Harrison had to feel the pounding of her pulse, too— their bodies were so close, in so many places—but he didn't say a word. He only held her gaze tight with his and began to dance again, with all the grace and style of a *vaquero*. As the final notes of the song came to a close, he pulled her close one last time, and then—of course—he tilted her back until her head was nearly touching the floor, in a dip that was nothing short of spectacular.

At that point, they were both breathing heavily, a combination of both the dance and their heightened awareness of each other. They'd also earned an audience, Gracie realized, when she heard applause. Or maybe that was just in her own brain, acknowledging his skill at…oh, so many things, because she honestly wasn't even conscious of anyone in that moment but him.

Still poised in the dip, her free arm looped around his neck, she said breathlessly, "You've been holding out on me."

He grinned. But he didn't let her up. Instead he only roped his arm more possessively around her waist and pulled her closer to him. He, too, was out of breath, his voice quiet when he spoke. "My mother made me take cotillion classes when I was in middle school. I hated it until I realized how many points knowing how to dance earned me with girls. Knowing the tango multiplied those points by about a thousand."

"I can see how that would work in a guy's favor."

Still, he didn't let her up, and still, Gracie didn't care. For one interminable moment, it almost seemed as if he were bending his head closer to hers, as if his mouth were hovering over hers, as if he actually intended to—

She closed her eyes, and for the merest, faintest, most exquisite millisecond, she thought she felt the brush of his lips over hers. But when she opened her eyes, he was levering her to a standing position, so she told herself she'd only imagined it.

The crowd had dispersed, caught up in another song, another dance, another moment. But Gracie couldn't quite let this moment go. Their fingers were still curled together, her other hand still curved around his nape while his was still pressing into the small of her back. Although they'd stopped moving, she couldn't seem to catch her breath. And in spite of the music that still swirled around them, she couldn't seem to make herself move.

But neither, did it seem, could he. His breathing was as erratic as hers, and he wasn't any more inclined to move than she was. And that maybe-imaginary, maybe-not kiss still had her brain so muddled, she wasn't sure what to do. Even when he began to lower his head toward hers—there was no mistaking his intention this time—she didn't know how to react. Not until his mouth covered hers completely. After that, she knew exactly what to do.

She kissed him back.

The feel of his mouth on hers was extraordinary, at once entreating and demanding, tender and rough, soft and firm. He kissed her as if he had done it a million times and never before, confident of his effect on her and tentative in his reception. Gracie kept her hand cupped over his nape, and with the other, threaded her fingers into his hair. It had been so long since she had been this close to a man, so long since she had allowed herself to get lost in the sensation of two bodies struggling to become one. She didn't want it to stop. She wanted to stay here in this spot, with this man, forever.

By the time he pulled back, her brain was so rattled,

her body so incited, her senses so aroused, all she could do was say the first thing that popped into her head. "I thought you didn't like me."

He nuzzled the curve where her neck joined her shoulder. "Oh, I like you very much."

"You think I took advantage of your father."

He nipped her earlobe. Gracie tried not to swoon. "I don't think that at all."

"Since when?" she asked, her voice barely audible.

Instead of answering, he skimmed his lips lightly along her throat, her jaw, her temple. But just when she thought she would melt into a puddle of ruined womanhood at his feet, he straightened. And then he began to lead her in the tango again, as if nothing had happened.

Well, nothing except a major tilt of the earth's axis that had just changed *every*thing for Gracie.

It was that damned dress.

That was what Harrison told himself as he and Gracie sat on opposite sides of a cab as it sped down Hamilton Avenue, back toward their hotel. Someone somewhere had put a spell on that dress that made men's brains turn to pudding whenever they got within fifteen feet of it. And when it was on someone like Gracie, with creamy skin and silky hair and eyes dark enough for a man to lose himself in for days, well... It was amazing all he'd done on that dance floor was kiss her.

But he had kissed her. And he'd told her he liked her. Very much. But he hadn't been able to answer her question about "since when." Probably because he didn't know "since when."

When had that happened? Today at the storage unit?

Yesterday at the baseball game? That morning at the stock exchange? He honestly didn't know. He only knew he had been wrong about her. She really had been his father's friend and nothing more. She really was a decent person. She really was a girl next door.

Now he just had to figure out what to do. Almost since the moment they met, he'd been suspicious of her. But he'd also been attracted to her. He'd wanted to expose her as a fraud, but he'd also wanted to have sex with her. He'd been sure every word she said about his father was untrue, but he'd learned things about his father from her that he'd never known before.

Hell, no wonder he didn't know what to do.

Bottom line, he told himself. That was what everything came down to in life. What was the bottom line?

The bottom line was he liked Gracie. The bottom line was he wanted her. The bottom line was she'd kissed him back on that dance floor. The bottom line was she wanted him, too.

So why not do what he always did when he was attracted to a woman, and she was attracted to him? Once they got back to the hotel, they could have a nightcap and then hop into bed and enjoy themselves. No harm, no foul, a good time had by all. There was nothing in this encounter that was any different from any other encounter he'd had with a woman. Maybe the circumstances of their meeting were a little weirder, but the essentials were the same. Man, woman. Hormones, pheromones. Foreplay, play, replay. He'd done it a million times, a million ways, with a million women. So what was the problem?

He looked at Gracie again. She was staring out the window, the passing streetlights throwing her beautiful

face into light, then dark, then light, then dark. Maybe
that was the problem. All this time, he'd been trying
to focus on her dark side. Now he was seeing the light.
And he... Hell, there were times when he wondered if
he even had a light side.

What would happen if his dark side mingled with
Gracie's light side? Would it leave them both more bal-
anced? Or would it just turn everything gray?

As if he'd uttered the question out loud, she turned
to look at him. She really was beautiful, whether in
light or dark. And he really did want her. He just
wished he knew what the fallout of having her would
be. And that thought was strange, because he'd never
worried about fallout before.

Clearly, girls next door were a lot more dangerous
than con artists.

When they arrived back at Gracie's hotel room and
she turned to tell Harrison good-night, she could see
he was no more ready to say the words than she was.
In fact, the way he was looking at her now was a lot
like the way he'd looked just before he'd kissed her at
the Moondrop Ballroom. So it really didn't come as a
surprise when he took a step closer and dipped his head
to hers. Nor was it surprising when she took a step forward and tilted her head back to meet him.

The kiss was even better this time. Maybe because
Gracie played an equal part in it from the beginning, or
maybe because she had time to enjoy it from the very
start. Something about the feel of Harrison's mouth on
hers felt like coming home. But to a home where she
didn't have to live all by herself.

Reluctantly, she ended the kiss. "Do you… Um, do you want to come inside?"

He met her gaze intently. "Yeah. Are you sure you want me to?"

She nodded.

"Because if I come inside, Gracie, I won't leave until morning."

Actually, she was kind of hoping he wouldn't want to leave at all. But morning was good for a start. "That's okay," she told him. "I don't want you to leave." There. Let him make of that what he would.

He dipped his head forward in silent acknowledgment. Then he followed her into the room and closed the door behind them, taking care to tuck the Do Not Disturb notice into the key slot as he did.

She started to ask him if he wanted to order something from room service, a snack or a bottle of wine or a game of Jenga or anything that might slow this thing down. But he obviously didn't want to slow down, because he pulled her close, looped his arms around her waist and kissed her again. He brushed his lips lightly over hers, and then skimmed them along her jaw, her cheek, her temple. With each new caress, her pulse leaped higher. When she splayed her fingers open on his chest, she felt his heart thumping against her palm, every bit as ragged and rapid as her own. When his lips found hers again, he deepened the kiss, and she opened her mouth to invite him in.

As he kissed her, he scooted one hand from her waist to the top of her dress. He pulled the zipper down down down, until it stopped at the base of her fanny, and the dress fell completely open. Then she felt his warm hand on her naked skin, his fingers pressing into her, pushing her more closely against him. He traced the outline of her mouth with the tip of his tongue, and then darted it inside to explore more thoroughly. His fingers went exploring, too, down to the waistband of her panties, dipping lower until his palms were pressing into the tender flesh beneath.

Gracie tore her mouth from his at the contact, gasping for breath, wondering again if this was such a good idea. But when her gaze met his, when she saw how dark his eyes were with wanting, how ruddy his cheeks were with his desire, how damp his mouth was from her own, she moved her fingers to his shirt, carefully slipping the buttons from their fastenings, one by one.

Harrison watched, his own breath shallow and warm against her temple, his hands still where he'd left them, curving over her bare bottom. Her fingers began to tremble after the third button, but she managed to undo them all. He released her long enough to shrug out of his shirt and jacket at once, leaving him bare above the waist, an absolute feast for her eyes.

His torso was long and lean, his shoulders wide and rugged, all of him corded with muscle. Her hands were on him before she even made the decision to touch him, her palms flattening against his smooth flesh, her fingertips raking gentle lines along each salient ridge until she reached his shoulders. Then she ran her hands down over the bumps of biceps, triceps and everything that came after.

When she reached his wrists, he turned his hands so they were grasping hers, and then urged her arms down to her sides. With one deft move, he hooked his fingers in the sleeves of her dress and nudged them over her shoulders, tugging on the garment until it

pooled in a heap of frothy mint at her feet. Beneath
it, she wore only white lace panties and a strapless
bra. His gaze flew to the latter, followed by his hands.
Without hesitation, he cupped one over each breast,
making his claim to her absolute. Gracie fairly purred
at the contact, and then lifted her hands to his torso
again, touching him just as intimately. After squeez-
ing her breasts gently, he moved his hands to her back,
unhooking her bra to let it fall to the floor before pulling her body flush against his.

The sensation of finally touching him, flesh to
flesh, heat to heat, was breathtaking...literally. Gracie's
breath caught in her throat at the contact. He lowered
his head and kissed her again, driving a hand between
their bodies to grasp her breast once more. He moved
his thumb over her nipple several times, before cra-
dling her fully in his hand. She felt him swell to life
against her, getting harder with each touch, until he
was straining against his zipper. When she lowered her
hand to his fly, he began backing her toward the bed.
The action moved her hand more intimately against
him, making him harder still.

By the time they reached the bed, his pants were
open, and she was stroking him over the silk of his
boxers. He growled something unintelligible against
her mouth, and then sat down on the edge of the mattress, bringing her down on his lap to face him, her
legs straddling his. For a moment, he only held her
there with a hand on each hip, kissing her and kissing her and kissing her. Then he moved his mouth to
her breast and kissed her there, too. First one, then the
other, licking her, sucking her, driving her mad. Gracie twined her fingers in his hair and held him there,

relishing each new touch of his tongue. Then she felt his hand between her legs, pressing into her over her panties, gently rubbing her with one finger, then two, creating a delicious friction that nearly drove her mad.

And then he was pulling the fabric aside, pushing his fingers into the damp folds of her flesh, slipping one finger easily, deeply into her. Gracie cried out at the contact and instinctively tried to close her legs. But Harrison pushed his own wider, opening her more, making her even more accessible to him. For a long time, he fingered her, until she thought she would explode with wanting him. Only when her entire body shuddered with her orgasm did he slow his movements. And only when her body relaxed in her release did he let her rest.

For all of a minute.

Then he was rolling her onto her back on the bed and pulling down her panties, until she lay blissfully and wantonly naked. She sighed with much contentment and threw her arms above her head, dissolving into a pool of something sweet and hot. The sensation doubled when she opened her eyes and saw Harrison shedding his trousers, his cock fully erect and ready for...oh, anything.

When he lay down beside her, she closed her hand over him, dragging her fingers slowly down his heavy length and up again, palming the damp head before repeating her actions. He closed his eyes as she caressed him for long moments, his breathing deep and ragged, his body hard and tense. When she sensed he was close to coming, he grabbed her hand and stilled her motions, and then opened his eyes.

"Not yet," he murmured.

She started to object—she certainly hadn't stopped him—but he sat up and rolled on a condom. Then he pulled her up beside him, grabbed her by the waist and set her astride him again. As she draped her arms over his shoulders, he rubbed his cock against the wet flesh between her legs until he was as damp as she. Then he pushed himself inside her—deep, *deep* inside her. So deep, she wasn't sure where his body ended and hers began. Still gripping her hips, he pushed her up until he almost withdrew, and then urged her back downward. Over and over he entered her, seeming to go deeper with each stroke. Then he withdrew and levered both their bodies onto the mattress until Gracie was on her knees with her shoulders pressed to the mattress, and he was entering her again from behind.

She clutched the sheet in both hands, hanging on for dear life, knowing they were both close to coming now. Harrison rose up on his knees and held her hips, pulling her back toward him as he thrust forward, until finally, finally, both of them came.

For one long, lingering moment, it seemed as if neither of them would ever move again. Then he rolled onto his back beside her, and she straightened until her belly and breasts were flat against the bed. She felt his hand on her bottom, gently stroking her sensitive skin, and she somehow managed to move her own hand to his chest. The skin she encountered was hot and wet, his chest rising and falling with his patchy respiration. She turned her head to look at him, only to find him staring intently at her.

Neither of them said a word. For Gracie, that was because she had no idea what to say. Never, ever had it been like this with a man. No one had made her feel so desirable and so desired. She'd never felt the things Harrison made her feel and would never feel them with anyone else. She didn't know how she knew that, but she did. There was something between them, right here, right now, that was different from anything she'd ever known before. Anything she would ever know again. And she just wasn't sure how she felt about that.

Until he smiled. And she knew he felt it, too.

Only then could Gracie close her eyes and let sleep take her. For a little while, anyway. Because she knew she hadn't had nearly enough of Harrison. Not tonight. Not forever. She only hoped he felt that part, too.

Ten

Harrison awoke to a buzzing sound, and wasn't sure at first what it was. A hum of satisfaction after a night of unbelievably good sex? The fizzing of his brain when he recalled some of the finer moments of that sex? The thrum of his heart at the sight of Gracie, naked and rosy beside him?

She lay on her stomach, the sheet dipped low enough to reveal the expanse of her tantalizing back and the soft indention of the two perfect dimples over her ass. He stirred to life at the sight of them, and it was all he could do not to run his tongue down the length of her spine. He wanted to hear her make that sound again, that little gasp of delight when he moved his hand between her legs and dragged his little finger higher, inserting it softly and gently fingering the more sensitive, sultry part of her.

He bit back a groan at the memory and did his best to stifle the response of his erection. *Later*, he promised himself. After she was awake. They could both probably use a little more sleep. Even if he knew his body and brain both were done sleeping for a while.

He couldn't remember a morning after with a woman when he didn't want to race out of her bed or chase her out of his. Normally, at a moment like this, he was considering the scenario in the same way a jewel thief plans a heist, tracing his route from leaving the bed without waking his companion to completing his escape without setting off an alarm. At this point, he probably could be a jewel thief, so expert had he become at vanishing without detection.

But he didn't want to vanish this morning. And he kinda did want to wake his companion. And not just so they could have another round of riotous lovemaking, either. He was actually looking forward to having breakfast with her. Just the two of them, sharing coffee and toast and quiet conversation. And that, probably, was the weirdest thing of all. That he wanted more from Gracie than sex. He never wanted anything from a woman but sex. And once he'd had sex he seldom wanted a woman again. And breakfast? Conversation? Ah, no.

It finally dawned on him that the buzzing that had awoken him had come from his phone, lying on the nightstand beside him. He palmed it and held it up where he could see it. A text from a number he didn't recognize, one with a New York City area code. He thumbed the prompt and found a message from the private investigator his attorney had hired after the reading of his father's will. The one who was supposed to prove Gracie was the gold-digging con artist they'd all been so sure she was.

Damn, what a waste of money that turned out to be.

The text was short and to the point: Check your email.

In spite of Harrison's certainty that his original opinion about Gracie was wrong, something pinched in his chest when he read the message. He told himself that a terse direction to check his email meant nothing. The PI's initial report probably said something like "You're an idiot, Sage. The woman you hired me to expose as a predator is actually one of the nicest, most decent people in the world."

So why the pang in his chest? Why did he suddenly want to check his email? Why did he want to see a report if he already knew what it said?

He looked at Gracie again. She was still asleep. So, with all the stealth of a jewel thief, he eased himself out of bed, slipped on the hotel bathrobe he had shed a couple of hours ago and retreated to the other side of the room. He cracked the curtains enough to allow in a slice of morning sunlight, and then thumbed the email icon on his phone and waited. There were a lot of new messages, since he hadn't checked his mail since yesterday morning. Even so, his gaze flew immediately to the one from the PI. With a subject head of Re: Grace Sumner, the body of the email read, As per agreement, initial report attached. Information gathered to date. Harrison skittered the cursor over the link to the attachment. But something made him hesitate before clicking on it.

Would opening this file after last night constitute a violation of trust? He supposed it depended on what last night was. If it was just sex, then no, this wasn't a violation of trust, since no trust had been established. Sex and trust didn't go hand in hand unless the people having the sex had some kind of agreement. If they were married, for instance. Or if they had made a commitment or developed feelings for each other. Feelings of love, say.

None of those things applied to him and Gracie. Did they? They certainly weren't in love. They'd only known each other a week. And they really hadn't made a commitment to each other. Last night was just…

Well, he still wasn't sure what last night was. But even if he did feel different this morning from the way he usually felt after spending the night with a woman, there was no reason for him to hesitate. And hell, the PI's report probably just confirmed that she was on the up-and-up.

Before he could second-guess himself again, Harrison clicked on the attachment. Immediately, a document opened on his screen. And he began to read.

Gracie awoke slowly and squinted at the bedside clock, startled to discover it was after ten-thirty. She never slept this late. Of course, she'd never spent the night the way she spent last night, either. Harrison Sage was certainly a thorough lover. She stretched languidly and smiled at the pleasant stiffness in her muscles, marveling again at how quickly things between them had changed. Not that she was complaining—she liked this new direction. A lot.

Blame it on the ballroom, she thought with a happy sigh. Or on Harrison's sweet, wistful expression as he sorted through his father's things yesterday. Or on his

cheering for Roxanne at the top of the ninth inning and
his genuine delight when the Rockets won their game.
Or on their intimate conversation at the stock exchange,
or even those minutes in the library that first morning,
when he'd charmed her out of her anxiety. Those blue,
blue eyes. That luscious smile. That wounded soul.
How could she not fall for a guy like that?

Any rancor Harrison had shown since meeting her
had been the result of hurt and grief. Any chilliness
had come from his fear that she was taking advantage
of his family. Had the situation been reversed, had
Gracie been the one who'd lost her father and felt as if
Harrison were threatening her family, she would have
behaved the same way. They'd just needed to get to
know each other, to understand and trust each other.
Anything that had happened before last night didn't
matter now. Because all of that had changed. They
never could have been as good together as they were
last night if they didn't know, understand and trust
each other now. If they didn't care about each other.

And Gracie did care about Harrison. She cared
about him a lot.

She shrugged into the remaining hotel robe and
crossed the room to where he sat with his back to her,
reading something on his phone.

"Good morning," she said as she approached him.

He jumped up from the chair and spun around so
quickly, she might as well have fired off a shotgun. And
when she saw his face, something cool and distressing
settled in her belly. Because he didn't look as though
he thought it was a good morning at all.

"What's wrong?" she asked.

For a moment, he only stared at her, as if he were

searching for the words he wanted to say but had no idea where to find them. Or maybe he was searching for something else, something just as nebulous and elusive.

Finally, he pulled himself up until he was ramrod-straight and crossed his arms over his midsection as if trying to keep himself that way. "Two words," he said. "Wilson Braun."

Gracie's heart dropped at the mention of Devon's father. How on earth had Harrison heard about him? More to the point, *what* had Harrison heard about him?

"He's Devon's father," she said. "And like I said, anything that happened between me and Devon is in the past. You seemed to be okay with that. What does Wilson have to do with anything?"

Harrison studied her more intently, as if he'd been expecting a different reaction from her. "I was okay with the past when I thought Devon Braun was just an old boyfriend."

"He is just an old boyfriend." Among other things. Things Gracie preferred not to think—or talk—about.

"An old boyfriend you tried to extort a lot of money from."

The accusation washed over Gracie like a wave of polluted water. She closed her eyes in an effort to block it out, but that only made it worse. So that was what he'd heard about Wilson. The same thing a lot of other people had heard. Exactly what Wilson had wanted them to hear.

She opened her eyes again and met Harrison's gaze levelly. "That isn't true," she said, surprised by how calmly the words came out.

"My PI says it is," Harrison told her.

The PI, she remembered. The one his attorney had hired to prove Gracie was a predator who'd seduced an old man and stolen his fortune. The PI she'd been so certain wouldn't be a threat because her life was an open book. She should have realized he would eventually get to the chapter about Devon and his family. The problem was, he'd undoubtedly read a heavily edited version of the story—since Wilson Braun had made sure no one would ever hear the real one—and that was what he'd relayed to Harrison.

She sighed. "And of course you always trust people to tell the truth right off the bat, don't you?" The way he had with Gracie. Hah.

The charge had the desired effect. His brows arrowed downward and he looked less sure of himself. "He has no reason to lie."

"Maybe he's not lying. Maybe he's just misinformed." Hey, Gracie would give the PI the benefit of the doubt. She didn't like to jump to conclusions the way a lot of people obviously did. Even if there was a good chance the PI had been paid a pile of money by Wilson Braun to bury the truth like so many others.

Harrison's expression fell a bit more, as if it hadn't occurred to him that the PI could be wrong. Nevertheless, he said, "This guy doesn't make mistakes. He's one of the best in the business."

Yeah, so was Wilson Braun. At least, when it came to the business of silencing other people or smearing their reputations.

"What did your PI tell you?" she asked.

Harrison hesitated again before replying, "He spoke at length to Wilson Braun about your relationship with his son, and he sent me copies of emails from Wilson to you that indicate you tried to blackmail the family for six figures in exchange for your silence on the matter of an alleged assault Devon committed—a story that you manufactured in the hope of profiting from it."

The first part of Harrison's statement didn't surprise her. Devon's father had always made sure his emails were worded in such a way that they never quite sounded like what he was actually trying to do—bribe Gracie in exchange for recanting what she'd witnessed so the charges against his son would be dropped. It was money Gracie had refused to take. It was the second part of Harrison's statement, the part about him believing she would lie about something like that in order to pocket a pile of cash, that did surprise her. If after everything the two of them had shared, and after the way they had been together last night, he could go back to thinking the worst of her this easily and this quickly...

Very quietly, very evenly, she said, "The story wasn't manufactured. Devon tried to rape a friend of mine at a party. Thankfully, I walked in on it before it became an actual rape, otherwise that's what Devon would have been charged with, and that would have been the story his father would have been trying to suppress."

She paused, letting that sink in. Judging by the way Harrison's expression changed, it did. Some. So Gracie told him the rest of it.

"But Devon had beat her up pretty bad, so I took her to the hospital, and she filed a police report and told the cops what happened. I corroborated her story. Then Wilson Braun tried to bribe both of us to shut up and pretend it never happened. Did your PI find his emails to my friend, too?"

Harrison shook his head, still looking a little torn. "No. He was only interested in information on you."

"Then do you have copies of *my* emails in response to Devon's father?" she asked, already knowing the answer. If he'd read those, they wouldn't be having this conversation, because he'd already know the whole story.

He sounded even more uncertain when he responded, "He's working on it. Your old service provider won't release them without a warrant. Wilson Braun volunteered his."

"Yeah, I bet he did. He was super careful about what he said to me and my friend in his emails. Too bad neither of us was wearing a wire when he spoke to us in person. And he did everything he could to discredit us."

It was why the case had never gone anywhere and the charges were ultimately dismissed. Because the Brauns were one of Cincinnati's oldest and most revered families. They had more money and power than an entire Mount Olympus full of gods. People like that thought the world was at their disposal. They couldn't be bothered with things like the truth if it meant their perspective had to be changed or defended.

And Harrison was just like them, she realized. He'd decided a long time ago that Gracie was someone who couldn't be trusted and only cared about herself. And in spite of everything the two of them had shared, he'd gone right back to thinking that the minute he was given a chance. If his feelings for her were even a fraction of what hers were for him, he would never—could never—suspect her of doing what he was accusing her of now. He would trust her because he knew what kind of person she really was. Instead, when another mem-

ber of his tribe said Gracie Sumner was a liar, then by
all means, she must be a liar.

"You don't believe me, do you?" she asked anyway.

His expression revealed nothing of what he was
thinking or feeling. Which probably told Gracie everything she needed to know. If he couldn't trust that
she was telling him the truth… If the past few days
hadn't changed the opinion he'd originally held of her…
If last night had meant nothing to him…

"I don't know what to believe," he said softly.

Yep. That was everything Gracie needed to know.

"You'd rather put your faith in a private investigator
who doesn't even have all the facts than in me. You'd
rather believe Wilson Braun, a man you've never even
met, than me."

"I didn't say that," he said.

She inhaled a deep breath and released it slowly.
"Yeah, you did."

How could she have been thinking he had changed?
How could she have been thinking she was falling in
love with him? Someone who couldn't be trusted and
only cared about himself.

"I think you should go," she said.

"But—"

"Now, Harrison."

Reluctantly, he gathered his clothes from the night
before and went into the bathroom to change. When he
came out again, his white tuxedo shirt hung unbuttoned
over his black trousers, and the rest of his clothes were
wadded in his hands. Gracie still stood where she'd
been before, her arms roped across her chest, feeling
colder than she'd ever felt in her life. When Harrison
stopped near her on his way to the door, looking as

though he wanted to say more, she only pointed toward it silently and turned her back. But when she heard the click of the latch, she called out to him over her shoulder one last time.

"Harrison."

He turned slowly, but said nothing.

"I'll have Mr. Tarrant send the documents to transfer ownership of the houses to Vivian to me in Seattle and return them to him as soon as possible. And I'll ask Vivian to ship anything I left at her house to me at home. There's no reason for me to go back to New York. Or to stay here in Cincinnati."

He paused for another moment, and then closed the door behind himself. Only then did Gracie allow herself to collapse into the chair he'd vacated. And only then did she allow her heart to break.

Harrison felt flummoxed when he got back to his own room, wondering if he'd just screwed up the best thing that ever happened to him.

No, he immediately told himself. There had been nothing to screw up. All he and Gracie had had was a single night of spectacular sex. And lots of good things had happened to him in his life. He had money and professional success. What could be better than those?

Now his PI had information that might just prove Gracie was the financial predator Harrison had suspected her of being from the outset, something that increased his chances of winning back his father's estate. And that was really good.

So why didn't any of that make him feel good? Why did he feel so bad?

The answer came to him immediately, but he didn't

much care for it. Maybe because, on some level, he actually wasn't convinced that Gracie was a financial predator. Maybe he'd been too quick to come to the conclusions he had.

He tossed his wadded-up clothing onto the still-made bed and fell onto the mattress. Then he pulled up his web browser on his phone and typed the name *Devon Braun* in quotations, along with the word *Cincinnati*.

The first hits that came up were for his Twitter and Facebook accounts. Harrison saw photographs of an innocuous-looking guy of above-average appearance who talked mostly about sports and a band Harrison hated. No red flags. Just some guy whose family happened to have a lot of money.

Scrolling down, he saw a link to a blog that covered Cincinnati crime called "Word on the Street." It was written by a local resident unaffiliated with law enforcement and clearly stated that it reported gossip, rumor and innuendo. Not exactly something that instilled great confidence.

But still interesting.

The piece was more than a year old and described a rape charge filed against the member of a prominent local family, indicating that it came after sexual assault and battery charges against him in another incident were dismissed. Neither of the victims was named. Nor was the perpetrator. So why had this item come up in a search for Devon Braun?

Maybe because the author of the piece had hidden his name on the site somewhere so that it would still appear in searches for Devon but avoid the wrath of Wilson Braun?

If that was the case, if Devon Braun had committed these crimes and the charges against him had been buried, then there was still a criminal on the loose in Cincinnati, which was a scary enough thought in itself. But somehow even scarier was the thought that maybe Gracie had been telling the truth all along and really was the best thing that had ever happened to him.

And scariest of all was the thought that Harrison had screwed that up. Bad.

The feeling only grew stronger when he was back in his Flatiron District high-rise with the boxes from the storage shed he'd brought with him. The cartons were dented and misshapen from the trip, and each bore numerous Sharpie markings, in different colors and handwriting—his father's, Gracie's and his own.

They looked completely out of place in Harrison's bedroom, with its wall of windows offering spectacular views of the nighttime skyline, its sleek, tailored furnishings and monochromatic taupe decor. They didn't look anything like Harrison or the man he remembered as his father. They looked a lot like Gracie, actually, offbeat and colorful and full of character. They looked as if they belonged to someone who had spent their life, well, living. Yet they were set against the backdrop of a room that looked as if it belonged to someone who hadn't lived at all.

Was that how he seemed? Like someone who had never lived? Sure, he spent the majority of his days— and sometimes his evenings—in his office or someone else's. And okay, most of his socializing had something to do with work. But that was what a person had to do to build a successful life. All Harrison had required of his home was that it look like it belonged to a successful, wealthy man, because those were the adjectives he'd wanted attached to himself. His place had always reinforced that desire.

So why did he suddenly feel kind of useless and needy?

The boxes, he decided, could wait. Unfortunately, he couldn't find enough space in any of his closets to stow them. So he shoved them into the corner of his bedroom, where they'd be—mostly—out of view. Funny, though, how his gaze kept straying to them all the same.

Work, he reminded himself. He had a ton of it to catch up on before he went back to the office tomorrow.

He started a pot of coffee, headed to his office and pulled up his email. Then he scrolled to the one he'd received from his PI this morning. Then he hit Reply and started typing. But he didn't ask for more information about Gracie. Instead, Harrison asked for more information about Devon and Wilson Braun. And he made sure, before he hit Send, that he tagged it "highest priority."

It was nearly two weeks before he received a reply—at 8:13 on a Tuesday night, thirteen days, eight hours and thirty-seven minutes after calling Gracie Sumner a liar in Cincinnati.

Not that he was counting or anything.

And not that he hadn't replayed nearly every minute the two of them spent together during that time—like Gracie's shy smile that first day in the library, and how the wind played with her hair during breakfast, and her chirpy "batter, batter, batter, suh-wing, batter" support of the Rockets, and their chaste but mind-scrambling kiss in the Moondrop Ballroom. And not that, with each passing day, he'd become more convinced that he'd had something with her he would never find again and had completely, irrevocably screwed it up.

Because even before emailing his PI, on some primal level, Harrison had known he was wrong about Gracie and should never have accused her of lying. Especially after the night they'd spent together. He'd just been so stunned—and, okay, kind of terrified—by the speed and intensity of his response to her. So he'd looked for the quickest, easiest way to escape. The PI's report had offered the perfect excuse to put Gracie at arm's length again. Hell, arm's length? He'd sent her to the other side of the planet.

And then he began to worry that there was nothing he could say or do to repair things. That even if he did, Gracie might not forgive him or take him back. That he'd spend the rest of his life thinking about how happy they could have been together. How happy *he* could have been. If only he hadn't jumped to some stupid conclusion that ruined everything.

In spite of all that, Harrison clicked on the file from his PI. And immediately realized that yep, he was a first-class, numero-uno, see-exhibit-A jerk. Because Gracie had indeed told him the truth about Devon Braun. All of it. The assault on her friend, the police report, Wilson Braun's bribes to suppress it. And Gracie Sumner's refusal of the money he'd offered her.

Harrison grabbed a sharp knife from the kitchen and headed for his bedroom. He pushed a chair into the corner where he'd stacked the boxes from Cincinnati, and stabbed the packing tape seam of one to open it. He wasn't sure why he suddenly wanted—needed—to go through his father's things. Maybe because they were the only link he had to Gracie, and he just wanted to touch something she had touched herself.

His grandmother's five journals sat on top. She'd written the first entry the day his grandfather proposed to her and the last the day she abandoned her family in Cincinnati. Harrison had skimmed the first two diaries that day in the storage unit, so he picked up the third, opening it and riffling through the pages to check the dates at the top of each. Toward the end, he found an envelope shoved between two pages.

There was no writing on the outside, and the flap wasn't sealed. Inside was a letter written in his father's hand, dated two years before his death. It started off "Dear Vivian..."

Harrison stopped reading there, telling himself he should give it to his mother. But he wasn't sure his mother would even want to read it. Still, he should probably let her decide. Then again, maybe he should read a little of it first, to make sure its contents wouldn't make her feel even worse about his father's behavior than she already did.

Dear Vivian, I hope you and Harrison are doing well.

Oh, sure, he thought. His father had been out of their lives for more than a decade, and they'd had no idea what made him leave or if they'd ever see him again. Why wouldn't they be doing well? He made himself read more.

I suppose that was a ridiculous sentiment, wasn't it? How could you and Harrison be doing well in the situation I created for you? Please, first, let me apologize for that. Then let me try to explain.

Harrison had never heard his father apologize for anything. Whenever he was wrong about something, Harrison Sage, Jr. had only made excuses. And he'd never felt the need to justify anything, either. Harrison kept reading.

And, wow, did he learn a lot.

The letter was long, chronicling everything his father had done since leaving New York and his reasons for doing so in the first place. How he'd begun to feel as if he didn't know himself anymore. How there was nothing left in him of the boy who had hoped to become a major-league baseball player. How his intention when he came to New York as a teenager was to make enough money to support himself and the family he hoped to have someday but how, once he'd started making money, he'd fallen under its spell, and had wanted to make more. And then more. And then more. How it had become something of an addiction that motivated every decision he made and eclipsed everything else in his life.

He'd thought the only way to break the addiction was to remove himself from its temptation. He hadn't meant to stay away from New York—or his family—for as long as he had. But with each passing week, then month, then year, it became harder for him to figure out how he could ever apologize and atone for his behavior. Eventually, he had come to the conclusion that it was too late to even try, and his wife and son would never take him back. He knew by then that Harrison had built a successful business and was outearning his father, so he'd be able to care for himself and his mother. They couldn't possibly need—or want—Harrison, Jr. after all this time.

That was why he had decided to leave his money to Gracie. Because he'd known that Vivian and Harrison wouldn't want anything he'd earned after he shunted them aside. He'd known Gracie would disperse the funds charitably, but, even more importantly, she would also give a sizable chunk of it to Vivian and Harrison. That was the only way he'd been sure they would accept any of his wealth. If it came from someone else. Someone like Gracie, who was the kindest, fairest, most generous person he'd ever met. In fact—

The letter ended there, midsentence, suggesting his father had wanted to say more. Why hadn't he finished the letter? More to the point, why hadn't he mailed it?

The answer to both questions was right there in the letter. His father had been convinced Harrison and his mother wanted nothing to do with him. He'd convinced himself that he couldn't make up for what he'd done, so there was no point in even trying.

And that kind of thinking was crazy. Harrison and his mother would have absolutely welcomed him back into their lives. It would have taken time—and, possibly, professional counseling—to put things back to rights, but hell, his father could have at least tried. It was never too late to ask for—or obtain—forgiveness or make amends. It was never too late to start over.

Harrison halted when he realized that so much of what his father had said in his letter mirrored what he himself had begun to fear about Gracie. His father had been sure he'd irreparably botched his relationship with the people he loved, so he hadn't even tried to fix it and lived the rest of his life alone.

Gracie was right. There really was a lot of his father in Harrison. The question was, did he want to end up the same way?

Eleven

"That should do it," Gracie said as she lifted her pen from the last of a dozen checks she had signed in a row. "For today, anyway."

Cassandra Nelson, the financial advisor Gracie had hired to help her distribute Harry's money, smiled. She reminded Gracie of Vivian Sage, with her always perfect silver hair and chic suits. Gracie was wearing a suit, too, a new one—well, new to her, anyway. It was a lavender Givenchy from the 1950s. A real Givenchy, not a knockoff, one of the few things she'd let herself purchase with some of the money Harry had insisted she spend on herself.

It had been nearly a month since she'd returned to Seattle, and she hadn't heard a word from Harrison. Vivian had written to thank Gracie for transferring the deeds to the Sage homes along with a sizable share of

Harry's estate, closing with her hope that Gracie would "come and visit us when you're in New York again." *Us*, not *me*, clearly including Harrison in the invitation.

Not that Harrison had had any part in doing the inviting, Gracie was certain. Vivian was just being polite. She clearly didn't know that her son still clung to the idea that Gracie was a crook even after she'd given away so much of Harry's money. It was only natural Vivian would include Harrison in an invitation to visit. And it was only natural for Gracie to decline.

Even if she still thought about him every day. Even if—she might as well admit it—she still cared for him.

"Philanthropy isn't for sissies," Cassandra said, jarring Gracie out of her thoughts. "People think all you do is throw around money. But there's a lot of work and paperwork that goes into it. Especially with an estate as large as Mr. Sage's."

"So I'm learning," Gracie replied.

Boy, was she learning. Not just about money and how to use it, but about how people reacted to you when you had access to that money. She'd received enough invitations to functions over the last few weeks to keep an army of billionaires busy. Already, she'd put three of Harry's billions to good use, for everything from endowing university chairs to bailing out failing mom-and-pop businesses.

"Now then," Cassandra said, "do you want to talk about your own future? Please?"

Ever since Gracie's first visit to the office, Cassandra had been badgering her about how much of Harry's money she was going to put aside for herself, to make sure she was covered for the rest of her life. But Gracie always stalled. Naturally, she did want to be covered for life, but she wasn't sure Cassandra's idea of what that meant mirrored her own.

Cassandra's focus would be on Gracie's financial needs, where Gracie was more concerned about intangible needs. Personal needs. Emotional needs. No amount of money could guarantee those. Harry's money hadn't exactly brought her any happiness so far. On the contrary. Not that she wouldn't keep some—Harry had insisted, after all—but tallying a specific amount wasn't something she wanted to think about. Not yet.

Before Harry's fortune, all Gracie had ever wanted was a job she enjoyed, friends to have her back, a decent place to live and a man who would love her till the end of time, the same way she would love him. Seriously, what more could anyone want or need beyond that?

But now, when she looked down the road to the future, there was only a curve around which she could see nothing. She told herself she must still have a destination, but she just didn't know what it was anymore. Or who it was with. If anyone.

Gracie bit back a sigh. "Cassandra, I promise I'll get to it before all this is done, okay?"

They made an appointment for their next meeting, and then Gracie left, to go…somewhere. She had no idea where. She'd quit her job at Café Destiné since Harry's generosity meant she could return to school full-time in the fall and earn her degree by December. So job hunting could wait until then. In the meantime, there was still most of summer to get through, and little to fill the weeks.

Her days since returning to Seattle had mostly been

filled with internet searches for places to donate Harry's money, reading and discovering British TV shows on Netflix. Maybe she should get a cat…

Finally, she decided to return to her apartment. Maybe she could check out the next episode of *Call the Midwife* or something. She was sorting through her mail when she topped the last stair to her floor, so she wasn't looking where she was going as she ambled forward. That was why she didn't notice the guy waiting by her front door until he'd placed his hands on her shoulders to prevent her from running into him. She leaped backward at the contact, her entire body on alert. Just as quickly, Harrison lifted his hands in surrender mode and apologized.

"I'm sorry," he said. But the expression on his face seemed to suggest he was sorry for a lot more than just startling her.

It was as if he'd been conjured by all the thinking she'd been doing about him, as if he were here because she'd somehow wished for it strongly enough. In spite of how things had ended between them, she'd found it impossible to stay angry with him. Harrison Sage III was a product of the world in which he'd grown up, one of deep wealth and shallow feeling, where people viewed each other as opportunities and commodities instead of human beings. Mostly, she was just sad. Not only about how things had turned out between them, but also about how he had to live in that world and didn't seem to know how to leave it.

"What are you doing here?" she asked.

He said nothing at first, only scanned her up and down, as if refreshing his memory of her. Then he said, "You cut your hair."

Her fingers flew to her slightly shorter tresses. "Just a trim."

"I like it."

"Thanks."

She studied him in return and realized he'd changed some, too. Not his expensive, tailored, dark-wash jeans or his crisp, white oxford shirt. But the fatigue in his eyes that hadn't been there before, and the shadow of uncertainty in his expression. Harrison Sage had been many things since Gracie had met him—from antagonistic and suspicious to adorable and sweet—but he'd never been uncertain. To see him that way now made her feel...

Well, actually, seeing him looking uncertain made her feel a little more sure of herself.

"So...what are you doing here?" she asked again.

He hesitated, then replied, "I finally had all of my father's things shipped to New York from Cincinnati."

That was good, Gracie thought. But she wasn't sure why he'd had to come all the way to Seattle to tell her that.

"And as I was unpacking everything in my mother's attic," he continued, "I realized there might be something in there that you wanted to keep for yourself. I mean, you never asked for anything—"

It was nice to hear him finally say what he should have known all along. Gracie really had never asked for anything. Not from the storage unit. Not from Harry's estate. Not from Harrison. Even though it would have been nice if Harrison had given her a little something—like his trust or his appreciation or...or his love.

"But I thought you might want a keepsake," he continued. "Something that would remind you of him. Of your time with him."

"Thanks, but I don't need any reminders," she said. She pointed to her forehead. "Everything I need to remember Harry is right here."

"Wow. You really didn't want anything from him, did you?"

"Only his friendship," she said. "Thanks for finally noticing."

He said nothing in response to that.

So Gracie asked again, a little more wearily this time, "What are you doing here, Harrison?"

He studied her again. "I came for you. If you'll have me."

She felt the same tingle of pleasure that wound through her that night at the Dewitts' party, when he told the butler that she was with him. Because this time, he said it in a way that was even more romantic and intimate. She said nothing in response, however. She wasn't *with him* now any more than she had been that night.

When she remained silent, he began to look even more fatigued and uncertain. And more panicky. "Gracie, I am so sorry about what happened in Cincinnati."

The apology surprised her. Even with him standing here, having traveled more than two thousand miles to offer it, she was amazed he didn't try to stall or use a "sorry, not sorry" euphemism. Then again, maybe he wasn't apologizing for their last conversation. An awful lot had happened when they were in Cincinnati. Maybe he was sorry the two of them had shared that delicious tango. Maybe he was sorry the two of them had made love. Maybe he was sorry for those three red velvet cupcakes at the Rockets game.

"I'm sorry I ever doubted you," he went on.

Oh. Okay. Well, that was a start.

"I'm sorry I thought… I'm sorry I made you feel like a—a…"

"A trashy, scheming, manipulative gold digger?" she supplied helpfully, harkening back to their first meeting.

"Yeah," he said sheepishly. "Like that. I'm sorry I was such a colossal jerk."

Better. But he wasn't quite done yet.

"I'm sorry I jumped to conclusions after reading the PI's report," he continued. "I never should have read the damned thing to begin with. Not after we—"

He halted before finishing. Not that she needed him to finish, since she knew perfectly well what he was referring to now. He shouldn't have read the report after the night the two of them spent together. After everything they'd experienced together. He should have trusted her instead. He was right about that and everything else. But the fact remained that he did do all those things, and that he didn't trust her. It was nice of him to apologize for that now, but…

"But you did doubt me," she said. "Even after—" Gracie couldn't quite put that night into words, either. So she hurriedly said, "And you did jump to—and cling to—conclusions. And you were a colossal jerk."

"I know. I'm sorry."

She didn't want to make him grovel—well, okay, she *did*, but she wouldn't, because that was the kind of thing people did in his world, not hers—so she told him, "Okay. I appreciate the apologies. Thank you."

He looked even more surprised by her capitulation than she'd been by his apology. "So you forgive me?"

She inhaled deeply and released the breath slowly. That was a tricky one. *Did* she forgive him? In spite of all of her thinking about him over the last month, the idea of forgiving him had never come up. Then she realized the reason for that. It was because she already had forgiven him. She wasn't sure when or why. Maybe she just hadn't wanted to be the kind of person who held a grudge. Nobody was perfect. Imperfection was part of being human.

"Yeah," she said. "I forgive you."

It didn't mean that everything was okay between them. It just meant that she was willing to listen to what he had to say.

So she asked one more time, "Why are you here, Harrison? If all you wanted to do was apologize, you could have texted me from New York and saved yourself a lot of money on plane fare. I know how important money is to you, after all."

He winced. "Gracie, that's not… It's just… I mean…" He expelled a frustrated sound. "Look, can we talk? Can I come in?"

She would have told herself there was no point in either of them saying anything else, but he had gone to some trouble and expense to get here. The least she could do was hear him out.

"Okay," she said. "We can talk."

She unlocked the door and entered her apartment, and then swept a hand toward the interior to silently invite Harrison in, too. He entered quickly, as if he feared she might slam the door in his face, and she told him to sit wherever he wanted.

She was reminded again of the day they met on Long Island and thought about how different things were here in her world. The view beyond her window wasn't of the ocean, but of another building across the street. Where the Sages' library had been filled with expensive collector's editions of books, her shelves were crammed with well-thumbed paperbacks. Instead of leather furniture, her sofa and lone chair were upholstered in a chintz floral long past being fashionable, and her coffee table was an old steamer trunk placed horizontally. Instead of lush, jewel-toned Aubussons, her hardwood floor sported a rubber-backed polyester area rug.

Harrison seated himself on the sofa, close enough to one side that it was clear he was making room for her on the other. Deliberately, Gracie chose the chair. His expression indicated he understood her decision and was resigned to it—for now. Even though he was the one who had asked if they could talk, the moment they were both seated, he fell silent.

So Gracie said, "What did you want to talk about?"

He threw her a look that indicated she should already know. And, of course, she did. But just because she didn't want to make him grovel didn't mean she was going to make this easy for him.

"Oh, I don't know," he said. "Maybe about developments in the Middle East? Or why we have to learn trigonometry in high school when we never actually use it in real life? Or how the music these kids listen to today is nothing but crap?"

Dammit, he was trying to be funny and charming like he was that first day in the library. She had to stop him before she started falling for him the way she did then.

"I choose trigonometry," she said. Because there was nothing funny or charming about math.

"Okay," he agreed. "But first, I want to talk about me and you."

Again he'd opted not to stall. How was she supposed to stay cool when he kept trying to get to the heart of things? To the heart of her?

"There is no me and you," she told him.

"There was," he retorted. "Before I screwed it all up."

She still wasn't prepared for him to go there so swiftly and candidly. She said nothing in response to his statement, but met his gaze levelly in a silent bid to go on.

"A couple of things," he began. "First, when I got back to New York, I had my PI look into Devon and Wilson Braun."

"Because you still didn't believe me," she said.

He shook his head. "That was what I told myself in Cincinnati, but I knew I was wrong to have mistrusted you before I even left your hotel room. I was just too stubborn and too stupid to admit it—to you or to myself. But we'll get to that. The reason I had my PI look into the Brauns was because I just wanted to make sure those guys got what was coming to them. And they will. My PI collected enough info on both Brauns— they're even worse than you thought—to cause them a lot of trouble for a long time. With the law, with their friends, with their jobs, you name it. Those guys are going to spend the rest of their lives in disgrace and dishonor, and, more than likely, prison. I told my guy to get all the info to whomever he could trust will do the right thing with it."

"Wow," she said. "Thank you, Harrison."

"Now then," he said. "About that morning in Cincinnati."

She couldn't quite stop herself, and replied, "The morning you called me a liar."

He started to deny it, and then seemed to realize it would be pointless. "There's something you have to understand about me, Gracie."

"What?"

He didn't hesitate at all this time. "I've never met anyone like you before."

That comment, too, surprised her. "But I'm a totally normal person. There are millions of people like me."

"Number one, no, there aren't. There's no one like you. And number two," he continued before she had a chance to say anything, "until you came along, I thought everyone in the world was like me. Because everyone I met *was* like me. Selfish, greedy takers who looked at every new opportunity, experience and acquaintance with the same question—what's in it for me? There was no reason for me to think you weren't like that, too. It never occurred to me that there were people in the world who wanted to help other people and make a difference. People like you and my father. Selflessness was an alien concept to me. To me, it made more sense that you would steal from my father than it did that he or you would give money to people who needed it."

She remembered how his father had taught him when he was still a child that money was more important than anything else. She remembered how he'd gone to a school for thirteen years that stressed financial success over any other kind of success. Lessons learned in childhood went deep, she knew. People could talk all they wanted about how when adults made stupid choices, they had to live with the consequences, never taking into account that those adult choices were based on childhood experiences. If someone was taught early on to choose money over happiness, then no one should be surprised when, as an adult, that person chose money over happiness.

"So when you told me you were going to give away my father's money," Harrison continued, "I didn't believe you. That didn't make sense to me. At least, it didn't until you took me to Cincinnati, and I saw how much my father meant to so many people. That's when I started to understand why he would want to give something back."

Dammit, he was doing it again. Being that sweet guy who made her fall in lo— Who had made her fall for him.

"That morning in Cincinnati, after we…" He hesitated again, but his gaze locked with hers. "I'd never felt the way I felt that morning, Gracie. Ever. Always before with women, I wanted to be gone before they woke up. But with you…" He smiled halfheartedly. "With you, I realized I never wanted to be with anyone else again."

There went the happy humming in her blood again. It was nice, having that back.

He continued, "And I guess I kind of panicked, when I understood what that meant. That I…had feelings for you…that I'd never had for anyone before.

That I wanted to see you again. Probably forever. That scared the hell out of me."

The humming thrummed louder. Faster.

"When I got the PI's report, and I read the lopsided version of what happened, it was easy for me to jump to the conclusion I did, because it meant I had an excuse for not wanting to wake up next to you every morning. It meant I didn't have to be in… It meant I didn't have to…care for you…the way I did. It gave me an excuse for going back to being the guy I was before. The one who didn't have to feel things. Life's a lot easier when you don't have to feel. Feeling is hard. And exhausting. And scary."

Oh, Harrison…

"But even after you were gone, I kept feeling. Every day. Every night. I couldn't stop thinking about you. But I didn't know what to say or do that would make up for what I did. I was afraid you'd never want to see me again after that. And I didn't blame you. I worried it would be pointless to apologize or to try to make up for it, figured you wouldn't talk to me if I tried. I started envisioning a horrible life without you. Then I found this."

He reached into his back pocket and withdrew an envelope. "It's a letter from my father I found in one of my grandmother's diaries. He wrote it to my mother two years before he died but never mailed it. You should read it, too."

Gracie balked. "But if it was meant for Vivian…"

"Mom's read it and doesn't mind my sharing it with you. It's important, Gracie."

Gingerly, she took the letter and read it in its entirety. When she looked up at Harrison again, it was with a heavy heart. "I can't believe he didn't think you and Vivian would forgive him."

"I can," Harrison said. "Because I thought you'd be the same way."

"But that's crazy."

"I know that now. But, clearly, I had a lot to learn about people. I still do. I just hope it's not too late. Because I don't want to end up like my father." He smiled. "Except for the part about where he got to spend the rest of his life with you."

Okay, that did it. Her heart was fully melted. Harrison must have realized that, because he smiled and scooted down to the other side of the couch. Close to Gracie, where his knee could gently touch hers. And even that tiny little contact made her feel better than she had in weeks. Four weeks, in fact. Four weeks, one day, three hours and twenty-seven minutes.

Not that she was counting or anything.

He lifted a hand and, after only a moment's hesitation, cupped it over her jaw. Unable to help herself, Gracie turned her head until his fingers were threaded in her hair, and then moved her hand to his cheek, too, loving the warmth under her palm. Her heart hammered faster when she remembered what happened the last time she touched him this way. His pupils expanded, his lips parted, his breath stilled. But he didn't move an inch.

So Gracie did.

She stood and took his hand in hers, and then led him to her bedroom. It was all the encouragement Harrison needed, because the moment she turned to look at him, he pulled her into his arms and covered her mouth with his. He kissed her lovingly, deeply, and for a very long time, cupping her jaws in both hands. Gracie splayed her fingers open on his chest, loving the feel of his heart racing against her hand, as rapidly as her own. After a moment, she moved her hands to the buttons of his shirt and began to unfasten them, her fingers sure and steady this time. He, in turn, dropped one of his hands to the single, oversized button on her jacket, freeing it and spreading the lapels open. He looked surprised to discover she wore only a bra beneath.

He was also more than a little aroused to discover that. Because he immediately freed his mouth from hers and skimmed the jacket over her shoulders to look at her. To help him in that respect, she reached behind herself to unzip her skirt, and let that, too, fall to the floor. The pale lavender lace bra and panties she wore were nearly transparent, leaving nothing to the imagination. When Harrison saw her effectively naked, he sucked in a deep breath and released it slowly.

"Is this the kind of thing you always have on under your clothes?"

He obviously remembered the lacy ensemble she'd been wearing in Cincinnati, and it was actually one of her more conservative sets. She nodded.

"This is the kind of thing you were wearing all those times I was with you in New York and Cincinnati?"

"Yeah," she said. "Except sometimes a little more revealing than this."

His eyes went wide at that. "You're not really much of a girl next door, are you?"

The question confused Gracie. "What do you mean?"

He only smiled and shook his head. "Nothing. Just…"

But he didn't finish. At least, not with words. Instead, he went back to unbuttoning his shirt and shrugged out of it, and then pulled Gracie close again... in a perfect tango hold, which meant really close, really intimate and really, really arousing. He danced her the few steps to her bed, and then spun her and dipped her deeply. As he nuzzled the place where her neck met her shoulder, he dragged a hand down the outside of her bare leg, lighting little fires all along the way. When he reached her calf, he moved his hand to the inside of her leg and drew it upward again, halting scant inches away from the hot, damp core of her.

Although Gracie caught her breath in anticipation of his touch there, she still gasped at the contact, so sure and steady were his fingers over the sheer fabric. Slowly, carefully, he righted them both to standing again, but he caressed her though her panties the entire time, and she was in no way steady on her feet. So he maneuvered their bodies until they were lying on the bed facing each other. He kissed her as he continued to stroke her, this time dipping his hand inside her panties, but Gracie somehow found the presence of mind to unfasten his belt and zipper. Then she tucked her hand inside his jeans and boxers to grasp him in her hand, rubbing him slowly up and down, too.

For long moments, they kissed and pleasured each other manually, their tongues darting in much the same way as their fingers. But when Gracie felt herself nearing an orgasm, she circled his wrist and withdrew his hand in an effort to slow the pace. He seemed to understand and used the opportunity to rise and shed what was left of his clothing. Gracie did likewise, and then bent over the bed to turn it down. Harrison was behind her naked body in a heartbeat, covering her breasts with his hands and moving his cock, already sheathed in a condom, between her legs to wreak havoc where his fingers had been before. She sighed as he caressed her breasts and thumbed her ripe nipples, guiding his hips forward and back to create a delicious friction for their bodies. When she bent forward more, he gripped her hips and entered her from behind, slow and slick and deep, again and again and again. But once more, he stopped before Gracie or he could climax, urging both of their bodies onto the bed.

When he turned to lie on his back, she sat astride him and began to move backward so that he could enter her again. But he halted her and instead pushed her body forward, more and more, until the heated core of her was poised above his head. Just as she realized his intent—and before she could prepare herself—he lowered her onto his mouth, pressing his tongue to the damp folds of flesh he had already incited to riot. Gracie was washed away to a place where her thoughts evaporated, and she could do nothing but feel…exquisitely, outrageously euphorically.

As his tongue lapped at her, he moved his hands to her bottom, curling his fingers into the cleft that bisected it, stroking her sensitive skin up and down, circling the delicate aureole at its base before darting away again. The sensations that rocked her every time he came close wound the hot coil inside her ever tighter. When he finally slipped a finger inside her there, moving his tongue inside her at the same time, she cried out. Never had she felt such a rush of heat or exhilaration. But as the cataclysms began to slow, Harrison tasted her again, deeper this time, and penetrated her again, deeper this time, and set off the waves of pleasure a second time.

She cried out again at the sensations rocking her. Harrison rolled her onto her back, gripping her ankles to spread her legs wide and drape them over his shoulders. Then he lifted her from the bed to drive himself deep inside her once more.

A third wave began to build inside Gracie as he bucked against her, climbing higher and higher, hotter and hotter, until she was crashing to the ground, and Harrison was right there with her. As they lay beside each other afterward, panting for breath and groping for coherent thought, she wondered if it would always be this way with them. If there would ever come a time when their lovemaking wasn't explosive and fierce, when they didn't feel so urgent and intense.

But all the thought did was make her smile. Somehow, she knew they would have lots of time together to discover each other. They would have lots of lovemaking. Lots of feelings. Lots of chances.

She looked at Harrison, lying beside her with his eyes closed, his hair damp, his chest rising and falling raggedly. A chance was all she'd wanted from him. And it was all she'd needed to give him in return.

"I love you, Harrison Sage," she said softly.

He opened his eyes and smiled. "I love you, Gracie Sumner."

Okay, maybe there was one other thing she'd wanted from him. Now she had that, too. And when it came to love, not even fourteen billion—yes, *billion* with a *b*—dollars stood a chance.

Epilogue

It was snowing on Roosevelt Avenue in the borough of Queens. The fat, frilly flakes danced to and fro around Gracie as she stood at the edge of a vacant lot that would soon be a pediatric clinic. Although it was early April, and the snow wasn't supposed to last for more than a day—a good thing in light of this afternoon's ground-breaking ceremony—Gracie liked seeing it. There was something promising about snow. Something clean. Something genuine. Something hopeful. Something that said everything was going to be just fine.

And everything was fine. The clinic was the last recipient of Harry Sagalowsky's billions. In the last ten months, she had spent his money on hundreds of projects and thousands of institutions that would affect millions of people. She'd traveled all over the country to participate in not only ground-breaking ceremonies, but also ribbon-cutting ceremonies. She'd visited preschools, elementary schools, high schools and colleges, attended meetings in churches and synagogues, temples and mosques. She'd even been invited to a couple of weddings and a barn-raising that had been facilitated by Harry's estate.

She had seen firsthand the good things money could do when it was placed in the right hands. Harry had been wrong about money causing the world's problems. Greed did that. Money properly spent could create a utopia. She hoped Harry was resting easily now, wherever he was.

"Not the best weather for a ground-breaking," Bennett Tarrant said from his position on her left.

He was elegantly bundled in an exquisitely tailored camel-hair overcoat, a paisley silk scarf tucked beneath the lapels. Gus Fiver was a mirror image of him, his own coat a few shades lighter, and Renny Twigg almost epitomized Gracie's initial impression of her as someone who should be working outdoors in flannel, wrapped as she was in a red-and-black-checked wool coat that was belted at the waist.

Gracie would have felt bland beside her in her own creamy Dior-style coat, circa 1950, if it hadn't been for the luscious way Harrison was looking at her—the same way he'd been looking at her since she'd come out of his bathroom wrapped in a towel this morning. And that was a weird thought, since she'd come out of his bathroom wrapped in a towel lots of times. So why was today any different?

He was another reason the last ten months had been so fine—and so hectic. Bicoastal relationships weren't the easiest thing to maintain. But she'd wanted to finish her degree in Seattle, and his business was in New York, so one of them had flown across the country almost every weekend. Or he'd flown to whatever event she was attending with Harry's money to join her. She sent up another silent thank-you to Harry for making that possible. Yes, he'd wanted her to buy a house on the water or go to Spain with some of his money, but using it to see a man who had become more important to her than anything had given Gracie a lot more happiness.

But she'd had her degree for more than two months and still didn't have a job. Of course, that could be because her work with Harry's money had intensified once her classes concluded. It could also be because her search for work in Seattle had been kind of halfhearted. Then again, her search for work anywhere had been kind of halfhearted. There were probably more positions in a big city like New York—and, truth be told, she'd applied for as many jobs here as she had in Seattle. But as good as things had been between her and Harrison—and as big a pain as it was living thousands of miles apart—neither had brought up the subject of taking things to the next level. Like living in the same city.

"I like the snow," Gracie said in response to Mr. Tarrant. "It's very pretty."

"I like it, too," Renny Twigg said from his other side. "It looks like wrapping paper on this big, beautiful gift that Harrison Sage is giving to the neighborhood."

Gee, Renny Twigg had something of a whimsical streak, Gracie thought. Maybe she really should be doing something besides working for a probate firm.

"I think they're about to begin," Bennett Tarrant said. "Shall we?"

The ground-breaking ceremony went off without a hitch. Gracie and Harrison laughed as they jabbed their shovels into the ground, fighting to get them deeper than a couple of inches into the frozen sod. Gracie even stepped up onto the top of the blade of her own shovel in an effort to drive it deeper. But all that did was send her teetering backward. Thankfully, Harrison was there to catch her. He set her on the ground beside him before returning both their shovels to the community leaders in charge.

Once all the thanks had been made and the farewells uttered, Tarrant, Fiver & Twigg returned to the big black Town Car that had brought them, and Gracie and Harrison headed for his. As they strode across the vacant lot, the snow began to fall harder around them, blurring the rest of the urban landscape, making her feel as if there were no one in the world but them. Harrison seemed to sense it, too, because he entwined his gloved fingers with hers.

"I heard you applied for a teaching position at my old school," he said. "Kindergarten. Starting this fall."

Dang. Busted.

"Well, the listing came up on LinkedIn," she said, "so I thought, what the hey. I mean, I've applied at schools all over the place," she added, fudging the truth a bit, since she hadn't applied for positions in, say, Nauru or Abu Dhabi—or anywhere else that wasn't Seattle or New York. "I probably won't get it, though, since I'm sure they want someone seasoned who feels the same way about education that they do."

She couldn't help adding, not quite under her breath, "More's the pity."

Harrison grinned. "I've spoken to the director about you. Seeing as I'm sitting on the board now and all, I have some pull there."

Gracie grinned back. "So then I guess I really can kiss that position goodbye, since you know the first thing I'd do is rally for art and music classes to be mandatory and for the uniforms to be eighty-sixed."

Harrison's grin grew broader. "You should be getting a call this week, actually. You could really shake things up there. Get 'em while they're young and teach them about the stuff that's really important. Not that I told the director that part. I just told her you're exactly the kind of teacher that place needs. And hey, you'll have an ally on the board."

Gracie chuckled. "Thanks, Harrison." Then she sobered. "Of course, that means I'll be moving to New York. Will that be a problem? For us, I mean?"

Now his expression turned confused. "How could that possibly be a problem for us? We'd finally both be in the same place at the same time for more than a few days."

She shrugged. "I know, but we haven't—"

"Of course, apartments are crazy expensive in Manhattan," he interjected. "Living there on a teacher's salary would be impossible."

Ah. So. Evidently, that "taking things to the next level" discussion was still on hold for a while, since anything she would be able to afford in New York was probably still going to land her in another state like Connecticut or New Jersey. Still, they'd at least be closer.

"Yeah, crazy expensive," he reiterated. "So it would probably be better if you move in with me."

Oh. Okay. So maybe they *were* going to talk about it?

"Or we could look for a new place together," he continued.

Wow. *Really* going to talk about it. At least, they would be, if Gracie wanted to jump in. At the moment, though, she wasn't sure what to say. Harrison clearly was, though.

"But you know," he said, "the school where you'll be working is pretty traditional. For now, anyway. They might frown on one of their kindergarten teachers living in sin."

So then maybe they *weren't* going to talk about it. Or take it to the next level. Never mind.

Harrison sighed with resignation. "So it might be best if you just marry me."

Before Gracie could say a word—he'd just skipped every level there was!—he withdrew a small velvet box from inside his coat and opened it. Nestled inside was a diamond ring. An old diamond ring. A modest diamond ring. An absolutely beautiful diamond ring. It was probably about a third of a carat, mounted on a white gold, filigreed setting, and it was dazzling amid the falling snow.

"It was my grandmother's," he said. "I found it in one of the shoe boxes where my dad stowed stuff. The minute I saw it, I thought of you. If anyone could make this represent happy memories instead of sad ones, it's you."

That, finally, made Gracie break her silence. "You

told me you finished going through your dad's things back in October."

"Yeah, I did."

"So you've been thinking about giving me this since then?"

"No, I found this in August. But you were so busy with school and my dad's estate, I didn't want to overwhelm you."

Overwhelm her? He'd overwhelmed her the minute she saw him.

He smiled again, a little less certainly this time. "So what do you say, Gracie? Will you marry me? Or should I have asked you sooner?"

Well, he could have asked her sooner, she supposed. But it was never too late for something like this. Then again, with Harry's money no longer a strain on her time, and with her starting a new job in a few months, and with Harrison just looking so gorgeous and being so wonderful...

"Your timing is perfect," she said.

Just like you, she thought.

"Just like you," he said.

"Just like us," she amended.

He smiled at that. As he removed the ring from the box, Gracie tugged the glove off her left hand. And when he slipped it over her third finger, it was... Well, it was perfect, too.

"I love you, Gracie Sumner," he said softly, pressing his forehead against hers.

"I love you, Harrison Sage," she replied.

As the snow continued to swirl around them, and as he covered her mouth with his, Gracie couldn't help thinking she'd been wrong about the clinic for which they'd just broken ground. It wasn't the last recipient of all that Harry left behind. Because she'd just received the last—and best—part of that herself.

* * * * *

If you loved this first Accidental Heirs book,
pick up these other billionaire books from
New York Times *bestselling author*
Elizabeth Bevarly

THE BILLIONAIRE GETS HIS WAY
CAUGHT IN THE BILLIONAIRE'S EMBRACE
MY FAIR BILLIONAIRE

Available now from Harlequin Desire!

If you're on Twitter, tell us what you think of
Harlequin Desire! #harlequindesire

SPECIAL EXCERPT FROM

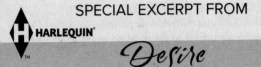

HARLEQUIN

Desire

*When the tycoon discovers that his enemy is pregnant
with his child, nothing will stop him from pursuing his
heir...and the woman he risks losing his heart to...*

Read on for a sneak peek at
PURSUED, the second story in
New York Times *bestselling author*
Tracy Wolff's
THE DIAMOND TYCOONS duet.

He was the most beautiful man she'd ever seen.

Desi Maddox knew that sounded excessive, melodramatic even, but the longer she stood there staring at him, the more convinced she became.

His emerald gaze met hers over the sea of people stretching between them and her knees trembled. Her heart raced and her palms grew damp with the force of her reaction to a man she'd never seen before and more than likely would never see again.

It was a deflating thought, and exactly what she needed to remind herself of what she was doing here among the best and brightest of San Diego's high society. Scoping out hot men was definitely not what her boss was paying her for. Unfortunately.

Wanting to free up her hands, she turned to place her glass on the empty tray of yet another passing waiter. As she turned back, though, her eyes once again met dark green ones. And, this time, the man they belonged to was only a couple of feet away.

She didn't know whether to run or rejoice.

In the end, she just stared—stupefied—up into his too-gorgeous face and tried to think of something to say that wouldn't make her sound like a total moron. Her usually quick mind was a blank, filled with nothing but images of high cheekbones. Shaggy black hair that fell over his forehead. Wickedly gleaming eyes. The sensuous mouth turned up in a wide, charming smile. Broad shoulders. And height. He was so tall she was forced to look up, despite the fact that she stood close to six feet in her four-inch heels.

"You look thirsty," he said, and—of course—his voice matched the rest of him. All deep and dark and husky and wickedly amused. "I'm Nic, by the way."

"I'm Desi." She held out her hand. He took it, but instead of shaking it as she'd expected, he held it as he gently stroked his thumb across the back.

It was so soft, so intimate, so not what she'd been expecting, that for long seconds she didn't know what to do. A tiny voice inside her was whispering for her to escape from the attraction holding them in thrall. But it was drowned out by the heat, the *sizzle*, that arced between them like lightning.

"Would you like to dance, Desi?" he asked.

She should say no. But even as the thought occurred to her, even knowing that she might very well get burned before the night was over, she nodded.

Don't miss PURSUED
by New York Times *bestselling author Tracy Wolff,*
available October 2015 wherever
Harlequin® Desire books and ebooks are sold.

www.Harlequin.com

JUST CAN'T GET ENOUGH?

Join our social communities
and talk to us online.

You will have access to the latest
news on upcoming titles and special
promotions, but most importantly,
you can talk to other fans about your
favorite Harlequin reads.

Harlequin.com/Community

Facebook.com/HarlequinBooks

Twitter.com/HarlequinBooks

Pinterest.com/HarlequinBooks

THE WORLD IS BETTER
WITH
Romance

Harlequin has everything from contemporary, passionate and heartwarming to suspenseful and inspirational stories.

Whatever your mood, we have a romance just for you!

Connect with us to find your next great read, special offers and more.